BLOOMING FLOWER RISING

Annette Greer

authorHOUSE®

AuthorHouse™
1663 Liberty Drive
Bloomington, IN 47403
www.authorhouse.com
Phone: 1 (800) 839-8640

Published by AuthorHouse   08/30/2016

ISBN: 978-1-5049-7588-9 (sc)
ISBN: 978-1-5049-7587-2 (hc)
ISBN: 978-1-5049-7671-8 (e)

Library of Congress Control Number: 2016914365

Print information available on the last page.

Any people depicted in stock imagery provided by Thinkstock are models, and such images are being used for illustrative purposes only. Certain stock imagery © Thinkstock.

This book is printed on acid-free paper.

CONTENTS

CHAPTER ONE

THE ALARM SYSTEM GOES OFF, and tells me it is morning. The alarm system is loud through the air, so loud that you can almost see it. It blares in and out with the wind. My G-Paw says it is the same alarm system used back in the olden days to warn us of weather conditions such as tornadoes or hurricanes. We now use the alarm systems in the morning hours to wake us; we have to, for there is no sunlight. The skies are dark and gray all the time. I pull myself up out of my bed, and in an instant, my censored room light comes on due to my body movement and my room becomes light from dark. I stretch my arms, and I crawl out of bed to head for the showers.

After my shower, I put on my school uniform, and I go downstairs to see if my brother, Jaybird, is up. He is, dressed and getting his breakfast administered to him already. He beat me, and he will get the better syringe today. My Momma is not home again. She travels a lot these days. She has to. She has to bring in money to buy all of our daily doses of food syringes. My Pappa stays home with Jaybird and me. He helps us get dressed, and he helps us learn at the learning center. He volunteers there while we are there. It is nice to see him every day. My G-maw sometimes tells me of a long time ago, when the parental segments were switched and all Mommas stayed home, and took care of the children, all Pappas went to work. Seems strange to me to think that that is how life used to be. It seems strange to me to see old, old videos of life so long ago. It is hard to picture how it was. I receive my daily dose of food injected into my side, and I am energized, and ready to go to the learning center with my brother. As we walk, we talk and hold hands, and we giggle. We have a great time walking to our learning center. It is not raining now, although the skies always look like they can open up and drench us at any time. Fortunately, pushing the special button on our backpacks provides us with a rain slicker immediately. The ground is always mushy, and wet, and there is a lot of sidewalk and concrete to walk on. My G-maw sometimes tells me of a long time ago when green, green grass covered the ground and the smell of the air was crisp; you could smell the scent of flowers, and hear birds in the sky. I would like to experience that someday in my lifetime. Experiment labs now generate the flowers. Few people get to see them. Studies are taking place in hopes that the flowers can live in our environment now. It has yet to happen. It has been so many years.

We get to the learning center, and the alarms finally die down, and we go up inside alongside the other children. Of course, that is a chore within itself. The other children make fun of my younger brother and me. I do not know why, they just always have. My hair is the color "blonde" and there are no other children in the learning center with blonde hair. Hair is usually dark in color, which is either brown or black. They call me a freak. I tell them that my G-paw tells me of a long time ago, when there were children that had my color of hair, many children. It was a common thing. There was abundant sunlight. There is no longer any sunlight, and to see blonde hair on someone is very strange and different to people. I guess that is why they call me a freak. My younger brother, Jaybird, was born with a sickness, it was cancer, and it was in his head. The Doctors tried to remove it, and they were successful, but left a large scar on his head, in addition, the other children make fun of him. It hurts his feelings, and he is my brother, so it hurts my feelings too. He is normal to me. To me, he just my Jaybird. I see him off to his class, and then I go to my classroom. I sit alone, and I see the other children stare at me. Sometimes I just want to shout at them, but I do not. It would just draw more attention to me. My Momma once told me to "turn the other cheek", whatever that means. I guess it was saying they used a long time ago. I do not think it would work now. I do turn my head from side to side, but the kids still stare. My learning center instructor comes in, and has everybody settle down, place his or her earphones on, and start watching the daily learning video. Our instructor's name is Ms. Goldenrod. She stays up front, and prepares for her long day of classes. As I try to watch my video on history, I can still hear the whispers of the other kids making fun and pointing at me. Ms. Goldenrod hears something and snaps her fingers loudly. We are all startled, and start trying to concentrate on our videos. I am safe for now.

After class, I make my way down the hall to my cube locker. In there is my snack syringe, which I decide not to administer for now, and a picture of Jaybird and me smiling, and posing for our G-Paw. It makes me smile to see it daily. All of a sudden, one of my classmates, Morning Glory, comes up behind me, and shoves me into my cube locker. Morning Glory is a tall, thin girl. Her arms look like long skinny vines I have seen in videos of plants, and her arms appear to reach out forever. The force of the impact makes me hit my head hard on the wall. I immediately swing around to see who did this to me. I can feel the warmth of the blood running down towards my nose, and I start to cry. It hurts and all I can see through the trickling blood are all the other kids laughing at me. My fists go up, and I start to swing at Morning Glory, but someone stops my hand. It is my best friend, Cardinal. He is one of my only true friends in, and out of school. His parents and my parents were friends in their school, so his family was always around. He turns me around, and starts leading me down the hall to find the nearest first aid kit. We do not have to walk far until we find one. By now, the blood is all over my learning center uniform, and on my face, arms, and legs. He reaches for some towels, and starts wiping me down. It is not the first time he has come to my rescue. He grabs the syringe that has the medicine in it, tells me that this will sting, and administers the medicine at the site of the cut on my head. I wince a little from the stinging medicine, and close my eyes waiting for the pain to subside. The bleeding stops and he walks me back to my cube locker. The crowd of laughing children are gone, and off to their next class.

"Blooming" he says", you have to watch your back! I might not always be here to rescue you! Morning Glory is out to get you! When I was younger, she was in one of my classes, and she always bugged me, and said she wanted to be my girlfriend. She would follow me home, and stare at me. It got so bad that my Momma had to go to the learning center, and make a complaint about her. I am afraid that she is capable to really hurt you or anyone"

"You are here this time," I say with a smile.

"Come on", he says. "I will walk you home."

I do not argue, but I do tell him that I have to get Jaybird first. I explain that I cannot go home without Jaybird. Pappa would be so upset if I leave Jaybird at the learning center on his own. He agrees and we walk to the office to summon Jaybird out of his class. We arrive at the office, and explain the situation, but Ms. Peacock, the secretary who works in the office can clearly see by my face that I need to go home. Cardinal speaks up, explains briefly, the confrontation between Morning Glory and me, and asks if he can walk me home safely, and then return to the learning center to finish out his day. Ms. Peacock calls Mr. Seagull, who is Cardinal and Morning Glory's instructor. Mr. Seagull agrees to let Cardinal walk me home, as long as he returns. She then proceeds to call Mr. Crow, who is Jaybird's instructor that we are heading down to Jaybirds class to sign Jaybird out, due to the circumstances. Meanwhile, in Mr. Crow's room, Mr. Crow receives the message and calls for Jaybird.

"Jaybird Rising?" he says loudly, and Jaybird looks up as if he was in trouble. "Jaybird, you must go to the office now."

All the other kids in Jaybird's class start chanting, "Jaybird's in trouble, Jaybird's in trouble." They laugh as he stands up, and slowly heads for the door.

Mr. Crow shouts, "Settle down! Jaybird is not in trouble and you all need to get back to your learning video!"

Cardinal and I appear in the doorway of Jaybird's room, and Jaybird slowly walks toward me, and then stops. My appearance scares him because there is so much blood still on my uniform, but I show him the cut on my head, and tell him that now our heads nearly match. I smile and reassure him that I am okay, and that we need to go home. He sees that Cardinal is with me, and I can tell the way Jaybird smiles at Cardinal, that being around Cardinal makes him feel safe.

On the way home, Jaybird walks ahead of Cardinal and me, and jumps into newly formed puddles from the dingy sidewalk below our feet. We just missed the daily rain.

"Why do the other kids treat me differently, Cardinal?" I ask.

"I don't know, Blooming, I wish I could answer that. Maybe it is because they are jealous."

"Why would they be jealous, Cardinal?"

"They are jealous of your family and jealous of the fact that your Momma gets to travel all over the world with my Momma selling gas masks," he says. "Our Mommas will be home soon, Blooming. When they come home, you know things are good, and our families get together in your parent's glass room and we all laugh as we learn of their trips, and travels."

We arrive at my house first. My house, as many houses in the neighborhood has no visible windows, and with all the rains, the black colored house looks as if someone poured black shiny paint on the house. The black paint is on all houses, because it is a specially designed waterproof paint to protect and seal the houses from water damage. The roof seems so steep that if you stand directly in front of the house, and look up, the roof looks like it is soaring straight into the dark charcoal colored sky. The rain slides off the roof, and it slants so rain does not gather to cause leaks in the houses. Cardinal leaves, and just as he turns to go, it starts to pour even harder. I see him flip his switch, and out pops his slicker. I turn and walk inside my warm, dry home.

CHAPTER TWO

WHEN I GOT INSIDE, I find G-paw with Jaybird in the common area of the house. G-Paw says, "I still can't get used to not having any windows built in these fancy weather houses. Why, back in my day, people would sit outside for hours, and watch the kids run up and down the street playing."

Jaybird curiously asks, "Didn't they all get wet G-Paw? Did they have to use their slickers?"

"No," says G-Paw, "it did not rain as much as it does today. In fact, there would be days, even weeks that there was no rain" He looked at me, and immediately sees the blood, and the cut on my head, and says "Blooming Flower Rising! What happened to you? Are you ok?"

I guess I had forgotten or a moment that I was covered in my own blood. "I am okay G-Paw; I will go get cleaned up."

I head upstairs to my sleeping quarters. I see that I have a message on my graphic communication interface. This is a machine that my G-paw and G-maw still have trouble using. They say when they were much younger, people used something called a computer, and watched something called a television. The graphic communication interface or G. C. I. was invented to eliminate both of those types of machines.

"I wonder whom that is," I say sarcastically. I slip off my learning center uniform, slip into my comfortable night clothing, and sit in front of my G. C. I. to see who has left me a message. It is a girl in my learning group named Amaryllis, a friend of Morning Glory's, of course. The message states in bold letters "We don't like your different colored hair, and you look like a freak! Morning Glory is not finished with you freak! She will pound your head into the wall even harder next time!

As I shut down the G. C. I., I roll my eyes in disgust. *Bullies! Both of them are nothing but bullies!* I think to myself. I have never done anything to either one of these girls. Amaryllis has always been friends with

Morning Glory. She has long, black hair, and she is and dark. I always thought she was beautiful, and wanted to look like her growing up, but she is a bully who just wants to hurt me. I decide to find comfort in G-Paw; I know he is probably tired, and ready to go to sleep. G-Maw is already in her sleeping quarters, and he is not far behind from joining her.

I position myself on the big, plush, comfortable couch. I sit next to G-Paw, and sitting on the other side of him is Jaybird playing with one of his action figures. G-Paw knows what was coming. We both yell, "Tell the story G-Paw!"

"Okay, okay," he says, with a smile, and we snuggle up close to him. "It all started back in 2015, the year the bees started dying. I was still a young lad. Bees were crucial for pollinating our fruit crops all around the world. Bees were responsible for pollinating 1/3 of our crops, such as blueberries."

"What did a bee look like? I ask curiously.

"Well," G-paw says", a bee was about the size of the end of my finger." Jaybird and I study G-Paw's finger closely as if it is the first human finger we have seen in our lives. "The bees were yellow and black, and had tiny, fast little wings, and made a *buzzzz* sound when they flew," he says. Then he makes a *zzzzz* sound with his old mouth, and his lips quiver as he makes the sound. Jaybird and I laugh aloud.

Jaybird says, "How old are you, G-Paw?"

"I am a very young 93 years old! I feel that I have the mind of a 20 year old! Back in the old days, back when I was born in 2009, your great G-paw, my Pappa, was what people called a 'farmer', and he would grow corn and soy beans in the rich, brown soil. There would be acres and acres of the crops as far as the eye could see. There would be sunlight to make the crops grow, and the sun felt so good on your face, and if you stayed in the sunlight for too long, it would make your skin tan and red." As I listened to my G-paw, I pictured how the crops must have looked, and I could almost feel the sunlight on my face.

Just then, we all heard the main G. C. I. ding, and we heard our Pappa's voice in the other room. We all three suddenly became quiet. We strained to hear the conversation, but we could not make out the words. After what seemed like forever, but was probably only a few minutes,

Pappa comes walking in to our area and says, "Mamma is coming home. She will be here in about two hours. She said if you both have been good, you would get a present!"

Jaybird squeals with joy, but I feel anxious from the day's earlier events, and I know my Momma will hear about what had happened to me for sure. There will be no present for me once she finds out. I do not dwell on that feeling much, because I am still very excited to see my Momma. I miss her because she travels so much for her work. She travels all over the world selling gas masks to people that are exposed to toxic air due to the sulfur leaking out of the ground during a sinkhole event. She and Cardinal's Momma work for the same gas mask company. My Momma has told me that when she was a young teenager at around the age of 15, the same age I am now, she remembers many changes the Earth went through due to the rains. Sometimes there would be sinkholes that would appear, and omit terrible toxic gasses in the air. People sometimes could not move out of their houses, so they started using gas masks to help them survive and breath. My Momma has an antique gas mask up in her living quarter's closet. I sometimes get a chair, and I climb up there and study it. If my Pappa ever caught me, I would be in some sort of trouble for sure!

CHAPTER THREE

I HEAD FOR MY LIVING QUARTERS and see that I have another message on the G.C.I. This time, it is a message from the learning center announcing the seasonal gathering dance. On the screen, I see a list of names that have responded with a check mark, confirming they were going to attend the upcoming dance. The dance was in July, just about a month away. I look at the names, and I see the name Violet Butyl. She is nice to me sometimes. I see Aster Manning, and I make a grimace. *She is a snob*, I thought. I do not know why the learning center calls it a "dance". No one dances; we just stand around and talk, mostly we talk about other students or what we are learning at the time. There are people that have signed the list as well. I see Cardinal's name, and my heart skipped a beat. I also see Goldfinch Hopper, and he is not a nice person. *I will not go near him if I go,* I think to myself. I also see Magpie Marks name. *He talks a lot.*

CHAPTER FOUR

After reading the list, I realize how tired I am, and lay down on my bed and I must have dozed off because I awake to Jaybird yelling, "Momma!" I quickly turn off the G.C.I., look in the mirror, and make sure I run a comb through my hair. My Momma always tells me that since my hair color is so special and unique, that I should always take pride in it, and try to keep it looking as nice as I can. She knows that in the past, I have been bullied for looking different from the other children. I rush down the stairs, and I feel that I am leaping down two to three stairs at a time to try to get to the foyer as quickly as possible to see my Momma. My Momma is standing there, holding Jaybird in her arms, and when she sees me, she opens her arms even wider to hug me as well. She smells of perfume. Rose Garden is the name of her perfume, and it is unmistakable. Her rain slicker is wet, and we have not given her a chance to take it off.

"Let me sit, kids," she says. Momma is so pretty. She has long, wavy brown hair, and a small petite body. Her clothes are always so modern, and she always stands up straight. I catch myself trying to stand up straight when I am around her, otherwise, my G-Maw notices and tells me to stand up straight. My Momma carries a large satchel on her shoulder, and we all know there are remnants of her most recent adventures in there. Pappa enters quietly in the room and kisses Momma on the cheek, and exposes a syringe he brought in from the kitchen.

"Thank you my love," she says to Pappa. "You always know what I need."

"It is the latest and newest nutrition they are selling at Mr. Raven's Market up the way. It was expensive, but I want you to have the best." Momma exposes her side by lifting her blouse and Pappa administers her syringe to her. She takes a deep breath, and smiles. Suddenly, I hear my stomach growl. It makes me hungry to watch her receive her syringe.

My Momma glances at me, and sees my head. I thought I had hidden the cut with my hair, but obviously, I did not do a very good job in doing so.

"Blooming, what happened now?"

"It wasn't my fault Mamma," I say quickly. "That stupid Morning Glory came up from behind me and slammed my head against a wall, while everyone watched." I see the scared look on Jaybird's face, and I feel my face turn red. "But I'm ok, really I am." I say. *I do not want to scare him any more today.*

Momma says, "We will talk privately later." She then heads for the common area and the big comfortable couch. Jaybird follows closely behind her. She sits down, and Jaybird sits right next to her.

"Jaybird," she says, "do you think I have something for you? Is that why you are sitting so close to me?" She grins, and then places her satchel on the floor, and we all grow quiet. We all know that she always tell stories about her travels, and she brings us the most amazing things.

She pulls out one of the gas masks that she sells, and it looks a bit smaller than what she usually sells. She tells us that this model is the latest and greatest.

Pappa says, "That is so small, how can that little thing keep all those deadly gases out?" Momma explains that this mask designed for small children, and it has been approved to sell in Asia. As Momma talked, I started daydreaming of lessons I had learned at the learning center about Asia. I remember learning about that country, and about the tragedy that hit Asia fifty-five years ago. The poisonous gases from the Earth at that time killed so many people that our armies had to go over there for fifteen years and help burn the bodies properly, as to not expose the healthy people from disease. Now, people young and old can use the gas masks, and are continuing to rebuild their communities all over the world. Over in Asia, I learned that people do not grow over three feet tall. This is due to all of the dangerous gas, spewing into the air, and over time, it has affected many people in Asia from being able to grow to a normal height. My family is lucky to live in the province of Hawaii. Here, the skies are gray and dark, and it does rain a lot, but not continuously, as in many places in the world, and the deadly sulfur gases emanating into the atmosphere causes dangerous sinkholes to appear out of nowhere around the Earth, sucking houses down into the sinkhole, and killing people. North America is a country that was once separated by states, and many years ago, numerous states were destroyed from deadly earthquakes. Thousands of people perished. We have provinces now. My family has always lived in the province of Hawaii, but my G-Paw and G-Maw met and lived in a state named Indiana many years ago. That is where his Pappa grew corn and soybeans. Today, people make a living selling things to keep other people alive. The corner market sells syringes for nutrition, and the newest rain slicker backpacks. There is a waterproof clothing store next to the market. Some markets sell home protection materials such as alarm systems. Some people in other parts of the world go hungry, and cannot afford syringes, and they try to steal things that do not belong to them. My Mamma told me that once, while on her travels, she came across a man that demanded her gas masks and nutritional syringes, but she pulled out her stun gun, and she had to use it on him. Down he went, and off she ran as fast as she could. My Mamma is so brave.

Mamma sees me daydreaming, and says "Bloom!"

I jumped back into reality and say "Yes Mamma?"

"Don't you want to see what I brought you?"

While on her travels, she went into an antique market, where they sell and collect all sorts of things from our past societies. She pulled out an 8 x 10 picture of a big, yellow dog. "Mamma! I love it!" I yelled. I remember learning of people owning pets, such as dogs and cats, and how many animals roamed the Earth freely, but they have been gone since long ago, and I may never see one in real life, but I see this picture, and I am amazed and happy.   Mamma said, "When people had pets, they would name them, and love them, and care for them".

"I will name her Sanctuary," I say. Jaybird waited impatiently for his gift, and she pulled out a model of a fighter jet from years ago. When the sinkholes started swallowing things up, the armies around the world tried several different things to make it stop, but nothing worked until the armies built these jets to fly over the sinkholes, and drop chemicals into the sinkholes to slow the progression. It worked, but the poison sulfur gases continued, and my Mamma started selling gas masks. Her

Mamma, my G-maw, sold gas masks, too. My G-maw does not talk about it much. I think she remembers bad things from back then, so we do not ask her about her past much.

Jaybird scoops up his present and starts running all over the common quarters yelling, "Take that you dirty sink hole!" and makes swooping motions with his model jet. Mamma announces how tired she is, so she and Pappa tell us to get ready for our sleeping quarters, and Jaybird and I head upstairs. As I head up, I look back, and saw the love in Pappa and Mamma's eyes, as they hold each other closely. That makes me feel good, and I jog the rest of the stairs feeling very content because everyone in my family is home. I am hoping to sleep well tonight. As I step into my sleeping quarters, I notice that I have messages on the G. C. I., but I am too tired to read them, and I slip on my sleeping clothes, and lay down in my bed, and fall fast asleep.

CHAPTER FIVE

W HEN I AWAKE, I HEAD downstairs, and realize I must have slept late because my syringe was sitting out on the counter. It was room temperature, so I know Pappa had to have set it out a while ago. I administer it quickly, and run around the house looking for Jaybird. I cannot find him, so I run back upstairs, get dressed, and decide to search for him. It is Saturday, so there is no learning center today. Jaybird is probably over at his friend's house, Chickadee McGee. Chickadee was a short boy, with a rather large nose, and he tends to be mean to Jaybird at times by teasing Jaybird about his scar on his head from the cancer. I run over to Chickadee's house, and see them playing in the back open area of Chickadee's home. It is not raining, but of course, it has been. They are playing with Jaybird's model jet on the cement block.

Chickadee yells, "Get that sink hole Jaybird! Make your jet fly down, and drop the chemicals into that sinkhole right there!" Chickadee points to an imaginary place on the gray, wet cement block.

"I'm getting it!" shouted Jaybird as he sways his arms wildly back and forth, tilting the jet towards the ground. I watch from a short distance by a dark corner of Chickadee's house. They do not see me. I love watching Jaybird play and have fun, just like any other child.

Just then, in pure, mean Chickadee McGee form, I see him touch Jaybird's scar on his head, and he says "Look Jaybird, your head looks like a sinkhole!" and laughed out loud.

Jaybird's whole body swings around toward Chickadee and shouts, "You take that back Chickadee McGee! My head does not look like a sinkhole!" He lay down his jet gently on the ground, and gets right up in Chickadee's face. "That is where I had my sickness the doctors call cancer, but the sickness is gone, and I'm cured, and my Mamma says that this scar on my head is to always remind me how special I am to be alive, so you take that back!"

"It makes you look weird, Jaybird" says Chickadee. My heart sinks, and I feel that I need to get Jaybird out of there, but I know that I might not always be here to protect Jaybird. Just then, it starts to rain again, and it is a downpour. The boys push their slicker buttons, and Jaybird shouts that he is not getting his fighter jet ruined from the rain, and he is going home. I sneak back around the corner so Jaybird cannot see me, and as I watch him disappear into the background of the dark skies. It is still early, so I decide to go visit my girlfriend, Daisy. She is not a close friend, but she is not mean to me like many other girls at the learning center. I head to her house, and the rain continually hits the top of my slicker. The rain sometimes smells and my Momma says it is the smell of sulfur, and that sulfur is a gas that fills the air all over the world from the sinkholes. If I smell the sulfur, I should use my gasmask. I immediately pull out my small gas mask from my backpack, and place it over my face just in case. I hop up to Daisy's front door, and knock. Her little brother, Wren, comes to the door, hollers loudly for Daisy, and disappears down a hallway. Daisy comes gliding down her stairs, stands at her door, and shouts "Hi".

I say, "Did you get the list of the upcoming dance last night?" I excitedly waited for her answer.

"Yes I did, and what are we going to wear! Get in here, and we will look up outfits on the G.C.I.!" I follow her in and I smell a scent in her house. Her Mamma had died about 2 years ago, due to the poison gases that she had to inhale for so many years while she worked outside for the province they lived in at the time. Daisy's family used to live in North America, in the province of North Dakota, and her Mamma worked in transportation business. Her Mamma worked outside, so she had been exposed continuously to the dangerous sulfur gasses, and she was eventually diagnosed of cancer. Daisy's Pappa immediately moved his whole family here to Hawaii to try to save her life with the most modern medicines available here, but it was too late. Her Mamma died here, and her Pappa decided to continue to live here. Her Pappa loved her Momma so much. Her name was Lavender, and he sent away for a little bottle of fake lavender scent to remind him of her. The scent fills the whole house, while it sits on a nearby table. I have never seen Daisy's Pappa smile. He always looks so sad. He must miss his wife so very much. Just then, he passes through the living quarters without even looking at me.

"We are going down to my sleeping quarters, Pappa!" yells Daisy, and off we go. I really do not think her Pappa is listening to her. Her Pappa does not seem to acknowledge her and his eyes stare straight ahead. Daisy's sleeping quarters were downstairs in her basement. It is very dark, until the sensor lights quickly come on as we walk in. It hurts my eyes a little because they were so bright. I blink quickly and try to get my eyes to adjust.

"I heard what happened yesterday," Daisy says. "You should stay away from Morning Glory and her friends"

"I was not around her." I say. "You know I don't have to do anything, and I still get picked on from her and her friends because of my hair color!"

"Your hair makes you a target you know. You can buy hair color at the market in the center of town, and make your hair black or brown, like the rest of us and you can blend in and not look so different than the rest of us," says Daisy. By now, her hands are on her hips as she speaks to me.

"What am I supposed to do?" I ask as my hands went straight into the air high above me." I will not change my hair just to be like everyone else! I like my blonde hair color, and my G-parents tell me it reminds them of how sunlight used to look!"

"We will never see sunlight, Blooming!" Daisy throws her hands up in the air as if she is surrendering the conversation, and plops down on her chair in front of her G.C.I. She quickly taps her hand on the chair next to her and motions me to sit down. We spend the next couple of hours looking at beautiful outfits online, and wishing we could buy them. We talk and daydream of looking so lovely at the dance with our beautiful new outfits, and everyone would stop and glance at us. We laugh and pretend that we are royalty in our new outfits. I lose track of time, and glance at her clock on her G. C. I., I see how late it is getting, and then I figure it is time to go home.

CHAPTER SIX

W HEN I GET HOME, I can smell my Mamma's perfume, and I know she is in the house somewhere. Jaybird is in his sleeping quarters, and G-Paw and G-Maw are running errands in the family vehicle. I know since my Mamma is home, we will have Cardinal and his Mamma over tonight for conversation. We usually do when Mamma is home. Cardinal's Mamma works with my Mamma traveling all over the world together selling gas masks. They have been friends and co-workers for many years as far back as I can remember. I walk into the living quarters, and see my Pappa sitting and reading his hand held G.C.I. "Hey Bloom", he says suddenly, when he notices I walk into the room, "come listen to this! According to the weather people, it will start raining here less frequently within the next couple of months, and the armies are experimenting with a new chemical to be released into the atmosphere above Europe, and if it works, they predict the rain will start to slow down, and maybe, just maybe the sun might come out! I know the government has been saying this for years, but Bloom, if this works, just think about it: your children might just see sunlight! There might be flowers and trees again for your children, and your children's children to enjoy! Your children might not know how dreary the world is. It might be dry and bright again!"

"Oh Pappa! How I wish I could see sunlight!" I say. "Pappa, why did you and Momma name me 'Blooming Flower'? All of my friends are named after flowers but me, and all the boys I know are named after birds, right?"

"That's right Bloom, and when you were born, you were so beautiful, and you had little wisps of light blonde hair on your tiny head. Your Momma and I could not decide on one flower to name you after, because you looked so unique, so we named you Blooming, because that is what all flowers do, they bloom into beautiful flowers, just as you are growing into a beautiful young lady!" He says. Pappa always knows what to say me to ease my mind. "Now how about you help me straighten things up for our guests tonight, huh?" So Pappa and I start to straighten the common area, and before we know it, everything looks to be in its place.

"I'm going to read some more world news on my G.C.I. to see what else our future holds, Bloom. These are exciting times we live in."

"Okay, Pappa" I say. I sit next to him and retrieve another hand held G.C.I on the table next to me, and I too start reading the world news. I enjoy the moment with my Pappa.

CHAPTER SEVEN

A N HOUR PASSES, AND THE doorbell rings. I am reading an article about different flowers the government is hoping to grow in the near future, and the doorbell startles me for a brief moment. I look around and Pappa is no longer sitting on the couch. I did not notice when he has left the room. I go to the door, and it is Cardinal and his Momma. His Mamma's name is Larkspur Miller.

"Hi Bloom." Cardinal says smiling, when I open the door. I love his smile, and I smile too.

Larkspur, Cardinal's Momma looks at me and says, "My, how you have shot up there, Bloom! Before long, you will be taller than me!" In addition, she lets out a big belly laugh.

Cardinal's Momma is not as tall as my Momma is, and her hair is very short and of course, brown. She carries some weight, but she looks strong. Her perfume smells good, but not as good as my Mamma's perfume. I lead them into the living quarters, and Jaybird comes flying down the stairs, excited to see our company has finally arrived.

"Cardinal!" He shouts, as he lunges into Cardinal's arms.

"Hi Jaybird," says Cardinal, as he catches Jaybird in midair. Soon, my Momma and Pappa walk in the room, and we all settle down on the couch and chairs.

"Hi Rose, did you see the latest?" says Larkspur.

My Momma replies, "No, I have been resting, and I have not checked my G.C.I today. What is the latest?"

"There is a new gas mask company over in Europe that is testing a machine that will supply people with gas masks when someone puts money into It.," says Larkspur.

Just then, my G-maw and G-paw appear from their sleeping quarters, and sit together on the loveseat. G-Paw overhears the conversation, as he walks slowly into the room, making sure he helps

G-maw sit down. "Sounds like what they used to call a bank machine back in the day. You could walk up to a machine, put in a code, and get money out. "He says.

"Well it will surely put us out of a job!" says Larkspur, as she shakes her head back and forth. Cardinal and I are quietly listening to conversation around us, and we smile at each other as we sit next to one another. Cardinal leans into me and says, "Grab your slicker, and let's head out to the back deck". I quickly and quietly get up, grab my slicker, and follow Cardinal outside. It is raining, but it did not smell of sulfur. We start walking down the sidewalk slowly, and he grabs my hand and holds it tightly in his. I decide to try to impress Cardinal with the recent world news my Pappa tells me earlier in the day.

"Did you know that there are new experiments in Europe, and if they work, we may see sunshine soon? What would you do Cardinal? What would you do in the sunshine?" I ask curiously.

He stops walking, turns to me, looks me in the eye, and says, "I would run to wherever you are, Bloom, and we would fall down on our backs, onto the ground, and just close our eyes, and feel the sunlight on our faces. That would be the best day of my life just to lay on that ground next to you, and feel the sunlight on our faces." He is smiling from ear to ear as he says it. I know that he really means it. Even though Cardinal and I have known each other for years, and he is my best friend, I see things in him that I never noticed before lately, and sometimes, when he talks to me, I get shivers. I do not know what that means, but I like being around Cardinal, and I think he likes being around me too. I feel safe around him, and when he is not around me, I miss him.

"What would you do if you see sunlight, Bloom?" He asks.

"I would run outside, and find you, too, Cardinal, and we would hold hands, and look up to the sky and laugh!" I say. I grab his hands, and start twirling around in circles with him. He eagerly joins in and we start twirling faster and faster, and l start to laugh, and so does he. We stop before we fall down from dizziness, and as our eyes meet, we grow quiet. "I want a flower garden if the sun comes out. I want a flower garden at my feet, and I want a little pathway in between the fragile flowers, so I can walk up to them without crushing them, and I want to smell them, and be surrounded by a sea of beautiful, sweet smelling flowers."

Cardinal leans into me with his whole body, and as he grows closer, I can feel his breath on my face. He closes his eyes, and without hesitation, I do the same. Our lips grow closer to each other, and as we almost kiss, we hear Jaybird scream "Help! Someone help me please!"

We stop suddenly, and start running to see what is wrong with Jaybird. We run toward his voice, and he is sobbing. "My jet is caught on the roof, right up there! I cannot reach it! It is gone forever!"

Cardinal is just tall enough to grab it, and gently glide it into Jaybird's hands as if the jet is flying. Jaybird calms down and says, "Thanks Cardinal!" and runs back inside, holding his jet close to his little body. Cardinal and I look at one another, and smile.

"Well, I bet they are ready to administer dinner syringes, Bloom. We had better go in."

"Yeah, I guess we should", I say, and I give him a half smile, and lead the way back into my house. Everyone is in the kitchen, and preparing the syringes for dinner. As we walk in, I keep my head down so no one will notice how red my face was from nearly kissing Cardinal for the first time.

Jaybird shouts, "I'm hungry!"

"Okay, Jaybird", Momma says. "Pappa is preparing the syringes as quickly as he can! Did you wash your sides everyone? We do not want to get infection again. Now, all of you go and wash up please!"

The three of us head to the two bathrooms on the other side of the house to wash the sides of our bodies from any dirt. We meet back into the kitchen and Pappa hands Cardinal and I our syringes. Cardinal reached for my syringe and says, "Here, let me help you, Bloom."

I expose my side, and allow Cardinal to administer my syringe. Then he picks up his own syringe, and administers it to himself. Jaybird exposes his side to Pappa, who is holding Jaybird's syringe, and says, "When can I do this myself, Pappa?

"One day, when you are a little older, Jaybird." says Pappa.

"Well," Larkspur says, "Rose, I will see you in two days, and we will go over our map to see where the company is sending us next".

"Okay, Larkspur," Momma says", Thank you for coming over, and it is always a pleasure to see you again Cardinal. "Cardinal nods in agreement, and off they go out the door, and into the rainy night. I watch at the door, as they get into their vehicle, and drive down the dark street, disappearing into the night.

CHAPTER EIGHT

A FTER THEY LEAVE, I SHUT the door behind me and I follow Momma into her sleeping quarters, and ask, "Momma, what happened to Cardinal's Pappa?"

"He was in the Army, Bloom, and he was a pilot, and his jet flew too close to a sinkhole, and the gases that spewed out of the sinkhole as he was flying over it exploded, and he lost control of his jet, and it crashed, killing him, and his 10 person crew. It happened in North America. I do not think Cardinal was old enough to remember, but he sure does look like his Pappa, that is for sure. I can tell you like Cardinal, Blooming. " Momma says.

"Momma, what do you mean? Like him how? Is she insinuating he could be my boyfriend, or something? Momma grins at me. I do not need a boyfriend, Momma, he is my best friend, and that is all!"

"Grab me my brush, please, off of my vanity, and I will brush your hair." As she speaks, she points to her vanity across the room. Momma says very calmly. "Bloom, my hope for you someday is to meet the right person for you, and have companionship forever."

"Like you and Pappa?" I ask.

"Yes, Bloom, like me and Pappa." While my Momma is talking to me, she is combing my hair, and every other stroke of the brush, a piece of my blonde hair would be stuck in the brush, and pull. I was doing everything I could not to wince in pain. I do enjoy these rare moments when it is just Momma and me, talking. "How is the learning center, Bloom?"

She knows about the learning center, and the incident between Morning Glory and me. "I know what happened, Bloom. Well, I heard something, I should say," says Momma. She always gives people the benefit of the doubt. She always tries to see the good in people. "Morning Glory really does like you as person, Bloom, she is just afraid."

"Afraid? Momma, she did not look afraid." I say as I lean forward so she can stop brushing my hair for a moment. "She came up behind me, shoved my head into my cube locker, and everyone laughed, Momma. Everyone laughed at me. Morning Glory would not have stopped punching me if it weren't for Cardinal showing up and saving me"

"Your hair color scares people, Bloom. People who allow their fear to guide them, such as Morning Glory does, cannot open up to possibilities in their lives. When you were a baby, and your hair started coming in, I knew that you were different. You have always been brave, caring, and kind. You are not afraid of being different, and you never have been. Remember when you were younger, and you were still in pre-learning center class, and your instructor was Ms. Carnation. That one boy, I forget his name--"

"It was Woodpecker Bentley, Momma" I interrupt. "I'll never forget his name."

"That boy would shout, 'Here comes that girl with the weird colored hair!', and you would just ignore him, but one day, you witnessed Woodpecker bullying another little girl, because she was born with only one arm, which made her appear different to everyone like you were. You heard him start to say mean things to her and you jumped over to them, and told him that even though her arm may never grow back, she will be okay, 'but Woodpecker, you will always be ugly!'. It shut him up immediately, and that little girl was safe for that moment. For that moment, she may not have felt different from everyone else. I bet she remembers you today, Bloom."

"Momma, do you have to leave in two days, can't you extend your home trip to three days please?"

"No, Bloom, I can't, Larkspur and I are being sent to Italy, but I know you have a big dance coming up in a couple of months. I plan on being back the day before your dance."

"How will we shop for an outfit for me, Momma? You won't be here." I say in a bit of a huff as I cross my arms tightly into my body.

"Now, Bloom you know that we can shop together via G.C.I., and if you find an outfit, send me a picture and it will be just as if I was right here with you. Look for something blue, Bloom, with a yellow pop to it.

The color blue always reminds me the reason your Pappa and I named you Blooming, instead of the particular name of a flower. When you were born, I looked into your eyes; you reminded me not just of one flower, but the beauty of all flowers as they bloom. That's why we named you Blooming Flower Rising." Just then, Mamma's personal G.C.I. chimes. A voice comes over her G.C.I, and says in a man's voice", Ms. Larkspur Miller is calling". That was Cardinal's Momma, and my Momma stands up, and pushes the accept button on her G.C.I, and walks away so she can have a private conversation.

CHAPTER NINE

I STAY AT MAMMA'S VANITY AND attempt to run the brush through my own hair, but it still hurt a little. *I do like my hair,* I think to myself, as I look at reflection in the mirror. I like how the blonde highlights shine in the light of my parent's room. I feel proud to be different, and because of Jaybird's cancer, and the scar on his head, he looks different too. As I brush my hair, sitting at Mamma's vanity where she keeps her perfume, and puts on her makeup, for a moment, I feel as pretty as Momma does. My mind wanders to a story Momma telling me the story when Jaybird was a baby, and she, and Pappa were preparing to travel to Pappa's relatives for a visit in the province of Texas. Texas is next to the ocean, and a long time ago, there was another province next to Texas named California, but after the great Earthquake of 2020, California fell into the ocean, killing thousands and thousands of people, and now there is just Texas. The air in North America is worse than it is here in Hawaii. It always has been. Momma says that at that time of their travel to Texas, I was here at home with G-Maw and G-Paw, because I was not feeling well, and it was during learning center season. Jaybird was no more a toddler, when his diagnosis of brain cancer was confirmed. Momma had been working for the gas mask company since I was a little girl. She had not started traveling at that time. The design of the gas masks were mainly for adults, but shortly after Momma started working for the company, she helped design a specific gas mask for smaller children. We have always worn gas masks, but I remember as a little child, gas masks were very uncomfortable. We were all so excited that we were going to be traveling all together, because that did not get to happen very often. I fell ill before our big trip, and had to stay home with my G-parents. I was feeling better within days, but my family stayed away for a long time. I found out that Jaybird was very sick, and I remember that I was so scared that I might not be able to see my little brother again. These days, I have friends, but no one tries to get too close to anyone because you never know who will get sick from the toxic gases that linger in the air, and then you might not see that person again. Throw in a girl that has blonde hair, while everyone everywhere has brown or black hair. Momma always tells me my hair is blonde because sunshine peered through the clouds while I was sleeping and touched my hair. There will come a time when Earth atmosphere settles down and it stops raining, the sun will shine, and flowers will once again cover the Earth. My G-paw and G- maw talk about the Earth, and how the Earth will be green again someday, and animals and birds will roam the Earth once more. I have only seen pictures and videos from the library archives of flowers and animals. I look at videos of flowers, and then fast-forward videos of the flowers blooming. It is amazing to watch plants turn into all of these wonderful colors exploding with lovely scents. I close my eyes sometimes, I can almost smell a flower, and it reminds me of how my Mamma's hair smells, which is sweet, and comforting.

Momma comes back into her room, where I was sitting, and tells me that Cardinals Momma, Larkspur, has some exciting news. Momma got her slicker, and left to go visit Larkspur. I have homework to do from the learning center, so I decide to get that done and over with. Tomorrow is Monday, and the weekend is almost over.

CHAPTER TEN

MOMMA WAKES ME UP THE next day, and kisses me goodbye. I give her a strong hug, and she goes down the hall and into Jaybird's room. Then I hear Jaybird cry, because Momma has to leave, so I trot down to his room, and try to comfort him. After I get him to calm down, we both dress into our uniforms. Jaybird and I head off to the learning center, and of course, the rain is coming down. Oh, how I wish the Sun would peek out for just five minutes on this gloomy, sad morning. *Maybe someday*, I think to myself. We arrive at the learning center, and I walk Jaybird to his class. I tell Jaybird to have a good day, and off to my class I go. I find my seat and try to slip in unnoticed. Our instructor announces that the science depot in town has gotten some hydroponic seeds of flowers, and in a couple of weeks, we all will get some. We are to place them in a special flowerpot that will be distributed to all students, with some special soil that will also be given to us, and if the sun ever comes out for even one hour, the special seeds will bloom, and maybe it can be the beginning of the Earth coming alive again. It has to start with the plants coming back. Scientists say that certain insects are lying dormant deep down in the ground just waiting for the sun to come out again, and then maybe the bees will come back. Oh, how I wish that I could someday see animals in real life instead of pictures or videos. The province of Hawaii, where we live, is the most likely place in the entire world to see sunlight first, because Hawaii is so close to the equator. I am so happy we live here. My Momma tells me stories sometimes of families she meets through her work, and how much harder those families live life. She says, unbelievably, in some places, the rain burns when it hits your skin. Many times, she and Larkspur have gotten sick from the poison sulfur in the air. I hope that does not happen again to my Momma. If my Momma were to get sick, I just do not know what I would do.

Class is almost over, and our Instructor gives us 10 minutes of free talk time. The topic, of course, is the upcoming dance. Everyone at the learning center is excited from the anticipation of the dance. There is a signup sheet circulating around class, and I decide to volunteer to help decorate the dance hall. I read that the first meeting is tomorrow after learning center, so I will be sure to go straight home to tell Pappa, so he can get Jaybird after class tomorrow. I barely speak to Jaybird as we walk home; I am too busy thinking of the dance. We arrive home, and Pappa is in the kitchen preparing the evening syringes.

"Hi Bloom, how was class today?" He says without even looking up from his chores.

"Oh Pappa!" I say excitedly. "We are going to get flower seeds from the science depot soon, and if we get just an hour of sunlight, they will bloom!"

"Yes, I know, Bloom. I helped on that committee. It was a surprise!" "I don't know what kind of flowers they are, but all learning centers here in Hawaii are getting them. The weathermen on the G.C.I. are saying that they expect a slight change in the weather in a couple of weeks, due to a change in the Earth axis of rotation. They are predicting that we may see a hint of sunlight here in Hawaii, but only here. If the Earth stays on this path and its current axis of rotation, we may start to see more sunlight sporadically throughout the year. This can change everything Bloom. You and Jaybird may have a better life than what I and your Momma, and even G-Maw and G-Paw have had. I want so much more for you and Jaybird, Bloom. I want you to have a good life, and I wish your Momma did not have to sell gas masks for a living. She sees so many sick people, and so much hardship. I hate that for her. She does it because she wants to help people, but I worry that she might get sick too." Pappa says.

"I worry too, Pappa. I wish she could stay home more."

"Well, enough sad talk, Bloom. Take your syringe, and go upstairs to your sleeping quarters so I can get this house straightened up please."

"Sure Pappa, I will." As I leave the room, I give him a big hug, he gently kisses me on my head, and I head upstairs to my sleeping quarters.

CHAPTER ELEVEN

As I enter my room, and can hear Jaybird playing with one of his toys, and I proceed to turn on my G.C.I, and there is a message from Morning Glory. It says, "We don't want freaks on our dance committee so don't show up tomorrow if you know what's good for you! You will get more of the same from the other day, and this time, no one will be able to save you. I will get you in a dark corner, and pull out all of your ugly blonde hair out with my bare hands you freak!"

I will show up if I want to, I thought to myself. As I thought this, I made fists with my hands and punched at the air above my head. I decide to save the message, and maybe I will show it to Pappa. This message is not like her other messages, and I am a little scared. I quickly save it, and turned on some videos of a comedy show to get my mind off Morning Glory. The comedy show is funny, and it makes me laugh. My G-parents watched comedy show a long ago. After it is over, I curl up into my bed, and daydream of the dance. At the dance, I walk in, and everyone turns to stare. I pretend that I hear some girls say how pretty I am, and how they wish they had my hair color. I see Cardinal, and he sees me. He walks over to me, and says, "Blooming Flower Rising, may I have this dance?" He twirls me on the dance floor, and everyone claps. Alas, it is just a daydream.

The next day, I could not wait for learning center to be over, and I head quickly to the dance hall to help decorate. Finch Carson is the first to greet me. He is a nice boy that always makes sure he smiles at everyone. I can see him being our class president someday.

"Hello, my name is Finch." He says.

"I know," I say", we were in the same class last year."

"Oh," he says. "Thanks for volunteering to help today. Would you like to pick out some paint?"

"Sure," I say. I pick out some orange colored paint, and I am pleased to see the theme of the dance is all sorts of flowers and birds. I start painting, and then I feel this cold glob of paint hit the back of my blouse with a thud! I whip around, and immediately see that it is Morning Glory standing there.

"You need to leave freak!" She screams. She has two other girls standing next to her, and by this time, everyone who is in the dance hall has stopped working on what they are doing, and is watching us. I feel my face turn blood red, and I am trying not to let my anger get the best of me.

"I have just as much right to be here as anyone!" I scream.

"Let's throw some brown paint on your head, and maybe you will fit in a little better!" Morning Glory grabs a brown paint bucket, and darts for me. She is bigger than I am, and she is too close to dodge. She grabs my arm, and she grabs it so hard, I think she will break it. She pulls me toward her, and proceeds to dump brown paint on my head. I try to pull away from her, and I am screaming, "Let go of me!" However, she holds tight. I start kicking her, and she finally releases me. Thick, brown paint covers me. My arm is hurting, and I can barely lift it. I look around and everyone is standing in a circle, just staring, and Morning Glory starts to laugh, and then everyone starts to laugh, and point at my head. I feel humiliated. I want to cry, but I do not. I hold my hurt arm with other arm, and I turn and look at Finch. He is supposed to be in charge, and I expect him to step in and at least order Morning Glory to the office for discipline. Finch is laughing with the rest of the crowd, and pointing at my head. I turn to see my friend Daisy. She is laughing too. Oh how I wish Cardinal would show up right about now. He does not, but my Pappa does. He appears out of nowhere, and guards me from the crowd of laughing students, and says "Okay, everybody, break it up! I will tell each one of your parents what has happened here today and none of you will be able to go to the dance!"

Everyone slowly started walking away, and as Morning Glory passes me, she shoves my back, and about knocks me over. I held my feet steady as best I could and let her pass. My Pappa stands in front of Morning Glory, and tells her that our family will be going to the authorities, and if my arm is hurt, her family will be paying the Doctor's bills. She looks at my Pappa, smirks at him and walks out of the dance hall.

"Come on Bloom, let's get you cleaned up". Pappa says. I slowly follow him to the washroom, and once I get out of sight of the crowd, I start to cry.

"Bloom, I'm so sorry that this happened. I wish there is something I can to make this all stop. After I get you cleaned up, I am taking you to the medical center and get your arm checked out. I can already see that it is bruising. We will go to the authorities on this, and Morning Glory could serve time at the Justice Hall for a while. No one has the right to hurt you like this, and get away with it. I saw her eyes, and she has no remorse. I am afraid she will really hurt you"

"I am not crying for myself, Pappa," I say. "I'm crying because I am sad that people can be this cruel to each other. I know they are scared because I look different, and I know that my name is different, but I am a person too, just like them. I have feelings, and I care about other people. I would never treat anyone like they treat me, Pappa, never!" I buried my head in his chest and sobbed as I have never sobbed before.

"I have never felt that you are different, Bloom, but what I have believed is that you are special, and you were born to make some sort of difference in the world because you are so unique. I love you so much, Bloom!" I look into my Pappas's tear filled eyes. I have never seen him cry. He hangs his head, and tries to turn a bit, so I cannot see his face, but I see how sad he is. His eyes are bloodshot, and tears slowly run down his cheek. My Pappa is very sad for me. At that moment, I feel very close to him.

He gets me cleaned up, and calls the office, arranges for Jaybird to go to a friend's home, while he takes me to the medical center to get my arm checked out. The Doctor at the medical center looks at my arm, and orders some tests to make sure it is not broken. He then steps out of the medical room, and comes back with the police. The two police officers ask me questions, and I tell them my story. The officers inform me that there will be an investigation of the incident. They explain that Morning Glory will face charges for harming me for no cause, she will be arrested and sent away, and she will not be able to hurt me any longer. The officers assure me that she will not be able to hurt me again. I feel hope for the first time in a long time that I will not have to be afraid of Morning Glory any more. The Doctors determine that my arm is not broke, and place a wrap on it where the very large bruise has now appeared. They gave me some medicine to help with the pain, and send us home. When I get home, I try to call Cardinal on my G.C.I, but I do not get an answer. I do not think too much about it, I am so tired from this horrible day, my arm is throbbing, so I take one of the pain pills the Doctor prescribes to me, and I curl up on my bed, and fall asleep.

CHAPTER TWELVE

THE NEXT MORNING, I GET up and hop into the shower. The hot water pours on my body, and as I look down, I see a bit of brown paint left in my hair wash down the drain. I see the paint run down the drain at my feet. I look at my arm, and try to convince myself that it feels and looks better today and I remember yesterday's horrible episode. I stand in the shower, and remember that I have not told Cardinal what has happened, and I feel a little worried that I have not heard from Cardinal. I hope I will see him at the learning center sometime today. I secretly hope that he will ask me to stand by him at the dance. I have been thinking more about Cardinal lately. I think about the other day when we almost kissed--at least, I think we were going to kiss. I ran through that moment again in my mind, but this time, as our lips grew closer together, we do kiss, and it was long and just the thought of kissing Cardinal gave me goosebumps all over my body.

What is going on? I think to myself. I get out of the shower, bandage my arm back up, and slip my uniform on. I rush downstairs to try to beat Jaybird from getting the fresh morning syringe. I go downstairs, and my Pappa is there ready for me. "How is your arm, Bloom?" he asks.

Just then, Jaybird comes racing into the kitchen, and says, "I'm here Pappa! I get to go first! Please Pappa! I'm so hungry today!"

"Okay Jaybird, I'm sure Bloom understands, right Bloom?" He asks, as he throws me a wink of his eye.

"I guess so." I say, and I wait patiently until it is my turn for my syringe. My Pappa has to administer my syringe to me, because of my arm, and Pappa is very gentle to me. He finishes up. Jaybird and I say our goodbyes, and Jaybird and I head to the learning center. Jaybird says, "Does your arm hurt? I know that Morning Glory hurt your arm, and the next time I see her, I'm gonna punch her!" "No, you can't do that, Jaybird. She is a very violent person, and the authorities will handle her for what she has done to me." I explain. "You need to stay away from her, do you hear me?" Jaybird looks at me, and knows I am serious, and nods his head yes. I get him to his class, and as I walk into my class, I see that Cardinal's chair is empty. Now I am worried. I do not see Cardinal all day, and I check to see if he leaves me any messages on my hand held G.C.I… but there is nothing. It is hard to concentrate on my lessons, and as soon as the day is over, I grab Jaybird, and we rush home. We arrive at our house, and the clouds above our heads look extremely dark today. I order Jaybird to go inside, and tell Pappa that I am running over to Cardinal's house for a moment. He says "OK" and runs into the house.

I walk over to Cardinal's house as fast as I can to see what was going on. I knock on the door, and someone I did not recognize answers the door. The man was tall and he sort of looks like Cardinal in the face.

"Hi, my name is Owl", he says. "I'm Cardinal's Uncle. I got into town last night. You must be blooming, right. Sorry, I don't mean to stare, but Cardinal told me you had different colored hair, I didn't expect it to look so light!" I feel my cheeks turn red from embarrassment. "Cardinal is not here right now, but I will tell him you stopped by when I see him, if you want me to."

"Sure," I say, "Is everything ok?"

"I'll leave that up to Cardinal, dear. Anything he wants you to know, he will need to tell you himself. Now if you will excuse me, I have young children to feed, and it is nice meeting you." He shuts the door, and I do not know what to make of all of this. I walk slowly home, and I just cannot help but feel something is terribly wrong. I feel helpless, and hope that Cardinal calls me soon. When I get home, I stare at my G.C.I. all night hoping that Cardinal will call.

CHAPTER THIRTEEN

THE NEXT MORNING, I GET up; check my G.C.I for any messages from Cardinal. The screen is empty. I hear Mamma's voice coming from the kitchen. *That is not possible*, I think. *She is away at work.* I get dressed as fast as I can and rush downstairs, and sure enough, my Momma is standing in the kitchen. My Pappa, and G-parents are also in the kitchen, and when I walk in, they all stop talking and look at me.

"Momma?" I say, "Why are you home, Momma?"

"Sit down, Bloom. I have something to tell you. Momma has a very sad look on her face, and I am not sure if I want to hear what she has to tell me. "It's about Larkspur, Bloom. She is very sick. She has cancer. The doctors can't cure her like they cured Jaybird."

"What does this mean, Momma?" I say frantically.

"Bloom, Larkspur is dying. We do not know how long she has, but it will be soon. Cardinal is at the hospital with her now, he has been, and he will not leave her side."

"No Momma, this can't be true! The doctors are wrong! They can fix her! I know they can. They fixed Jaybird, he is all better, and she will get better too! What will happen to Cardinal, Momma? His Momma is all he has!" I feel faint, and I sit down in the chair. Tears are streaming down my face, and as I look around the room, I notice that everyone has tears.

"Larkspur's brother is in town, and his family will be staying here for a while with Cardinal. They came from the Ohio province. That's where they live, and when Larkspur is no longer with us, then Cardinal will move to Ohio with his uncle Owl's family."

My heart sinks. I feel as if someone has kicked me in the stomach. I feel like my world is crashing down on me. I feel so bad for Cardinal. I have to get to him as quickly as I can. "Can I go see her, Momma? Please?"

"Not just yet, Bloom, you have to give the family space right now. Cardinal will need you to be strong for him. Cardinal has to be with his Momma right now while he can."

"How did this happen, Momma?" I try to stop crying for a moment.

"Well, the day we left," says Momma", Larkspur was so excited that they were sending us to a new province over in old Mexico to try out a new form of gas mask. This gas mask has not been on the market for very long, and I personally think it was not tested enough to be sold, but the company sometimes wants to get the newest product out to make money. The company sent us down there, and on the first day, getting off our Hover Plane, we could smell the sulfur thick in the air. I immediately put my gas mask on, but Larkspur put one of the new one's on. It had a leak in the hose, and she breathed in too much sulfur, Bloom. She started coughing, and I took her to the nearest Medical Center. They ran many tests and confirmed that she had inhaled too much toxic sulfur over the years. There is permanent damage to her lungs as well as cancer. The cancer is aggressive, and the Doctors can do nothing to save her. The Doctors will try to keep her comfortable, and try to manage her pain. The doctors said she more than likely had cancer already from years of exposure, but this episode brought it all to the surface. She has already gone blind in one eye, and is in an extreme amount of pain."

I start to sob, and I feel my legs give out from underneath me. How could this be happening! I think of Cardinal, and how he must be feeling. This is his Momma! How will he get through this? What can I do for him?

Momma reaches out and gently takes my face in her hands and says, "Bloom, she is my best friend", Tears are running down my Mamma's face, and she breaks down and falls into my arms. I hold her tight, and I can feel her whole body shake while she cries. I can feel the emotional pain she is in with each long, sad sob. Pappa steps in, and gently guides Momma to the couch. He gently administers a liquid syringe to Momma and she settles down a bit. We all sit in silence for what seems like forever. An hour passes and I hear my G.C.I. ring. I fly upstairs, and it is Cardinal.

"Oh, Cardinal!" I say. "I am so very sorry to hear about your Momma!"

Cardinal looks so scared. I have never seen him like this before. "Bloom, she looks so bad! I cannot help her, Bloom! I want to help her,

Bloom!" I see his lips start to quiver and his voice starts to crack, and then I see him start to cry. It was no ordinary cry. This is the most mournful cry I have ever heard in my life. I cannot believe this is happening.

"Is there anything I can do, Cardinal? I ask.

"Just pray, Bloom, pray that my Momma doesn't suffer." He starts to cry again, and hangs up.

I go downstairs, and run outside. I do not bother to get my slicker. I am too angry. The rain is coming down, and I look up at the dark skies, and start screaming. "Why!" I scream. "Why does it have to be her? She has never done anything wrong! Please don't let her die!"

I ask God to help her. I do not talk to God very much. After the fall out in 2015, churches became outdated. People lost a lot of hope, and quit going to church. Throughout time, churches have gone underground, so to speak, and people pray in private. When Jaybird became sick, I remember praying to God then and asking God to heal my brother. I feel that God did listen to me, and was there for Jaybird during his sickness. So now, I decide to ask God again to help Larkspur.

"Please God!" I say aloud. "Please heal her, and take her pain away!"

My Pappa comes out, and he hears me pray. "I didn't know you talked to God, Bloom. I am very happy to see you pray. I talk to God sometimes too. When your Momma goes away to work, I pray that she is kept safe, and so far, God has kept her safe."

"Then why didn't God keep Larkspur safe, Pappa?" I ask. "Why didn't he stop the sulfur from giving her cancer? Why is he so mean to her?"

"God is not mean to her, Bloom. God loves us all. God is very sad the way the Earth is right now, and he wants Earth to get better. He did not get Larkspur sick. He has no control over that. God watches over all of us, and I believe that he is trying to heal the whole Earth so that one day, there will no longer be any deadly sulfur to breath anymore. Larkspur, like your Momma, wanted to help people, and to try to improve their way of life. There is risk in everything. She knew of the risk she was taking every day, and so does your Momma. If we stand still, and do nothing, then life will pass us by, and life might not be worth living, but when we move and try to help one another, then that makes life worth living even if terrible things happen."

CHAPTER FOURTEEN

THE NEXT FEW DAYS ARE a blur. It is hard to concentrate on my studies, and Cardinal is able to do his studies from the medical center where his Momma is. He will not leave her side. He stays there day and night. One day, after the learning center, I try to volunteer to work on the dance hall decorations, but my heart is not into it, and I leave. I speak with Cardinal every night on my G.C.I., and he looks so bad. He has deep, dark circles under his eyes, and I know he is not sleeping much. I let him talk most of the time, and I just listen. One night, he says that his Momma had a good day that day, and she smiled, talked, and was able to tolerate a nutrition syringe without feeling nauseous.

"Maybe she is getting better, Cardinal!" I say with a hopeful voice.

"Yeah, maybe, Bloom. Maybe she will be cured, and we can go to the dance and stand next to each other and you can be my girlfriend."

Did I just hear that? I think. *Surely, he can see my heart pounding out of my chest through the G.C.I. Oh my gosh!* He just asked me to be his girlfriend! "Yes, of course, Cardinal!" I say excitedly.

Three days later, Cardinal's Momma passes away while she sleeps. Cardinal is right by her side, holding her hand as she slips away. Pappa tells me that Momma is coming home to attend the funeral. We are all going to pay our respects.

CHAPTER FIFTEEN

THE FUNERAL FOR CARDINAL'S MOMMA is very sad. There are many people there from Mamma's gas mask company, and they all came up one by one to Jaybird and me and told us how big we both have gotten since they have seen the both of us. I entertain Jaybird the best I could, and I am not sure if he really understood what is going on anyway.

"Why is Cardinal's Momma sleeping so much, Blooming?" He asks inquisitively.

"She has gone to heaven, Jaybird. She is with Cardinal's Pappa who is already in Heaven." I reply.

"Will Momma and Pappa go to heaven someday, Bloom?" he asks.

"Yes, Jaybird, they will, but not for a long, long time from now, so you don't need to think of these things right now." I say.

The funeral ends, and we all go back to Cardinal's house for a visit. It is a quiet, rainy day. Everyone is very somber. Cardinal is especially quiet, and I approach him slowly. His eyes tear up, and he holds out his hands for me. I quickly respond, and we hug for what seems a lifetime. Neither one of us speak to one another, because there are no words to say. After what seems to be forever, I say

"I am so sorry, Cardinal. I can't imagine what you are feeling, but I will always be here for you."

"Thanks, Bloom, I need to hear that. Did you hear that I have to move away with my Uncle Owl? He lives in the Province of Ohio, and I know that there will be a whole ocean between us, but he said we would not be moving until after the dance. It will take a while to get things financially squared away. Do you still want to stand next to me and be my girlfriend?" He asks.

"Yes of course, Cardinal, I wouldn't want to stand next to anyone else!" I say. I look straight into his eyes, and we stare at one another as if we are the only two people around.

The G.C.I. rings and it is the funeral facility ready to transport Cardinal's Momma to the holding building. When people pass away, they are stored in the holding building. Once a month, the departed are loaded onto a special space bus with permission from the families, and are transported to the planet Mars. Many years ago, the government traveled to Mars to see if life could be sustainable there. The Mars atmosphere was unable to accommodate human life, but the government sent probes to study the atmosphere, and soil on Mars. On one particular trip, the government did discover that the ground on Mars soil is soft on top, and then deeper under the many soil layers, the ground is hard. At that time, the Earth was running out of room for cemeteries, and the Earth was running out of places to bury people that pass away. People pay money for their loved ones to be transported to Mars for burial. Mars turned out to be the number one planet to send our loved ones that pass away, and it frees up places on Earth to build more houses because of over population.

CHAPTER SIXTEEN

THE NEXT FEW DAYS ARE as good as to be expected. Cardinal and I spend a lot of time with each other. We sit mostly on his porch and talk about his Momma, and watch the rainfall.

"Once," Cardinal says. "Momma always liked to try to play practical jokes on me, and I tried to play them on her too. We were always trying to outdo each other, and one time, she dressed up like some sort of scary creature, and snuck in my sleeping quarters and tried to scare me. She made a scratching noise. I heard it and looked under my bed. There she was, and I let out a scream! She laughed so hard! Then I started to laugh, and to this day, I think about that time, and I still laugh aloud. My Momma was always trying to make life fun for me, and I think because it was just her and me. I do not really remember my Pappa. I told my Momma I did remember him, because I think she wanted me to remember him so badly. I told her I did, to make her feel better. Besides you, Bloom, my Momma was my best friend." He says sadly.

We both look up to the sky, because the rain stops, and the clouds are moving quickly across the sky. It looks very ominous. We both look at each other, and we hope for a brief second, we are going to see sunshine! The skies quickly turn dark again, and the rain starts back up.

Cardinal swings his chair around towards me and says, "It's going to happen, Bloom, and when it does, I want to be with you, so it better happen soon". He sighs.

I think to myself that would be the greatest thing to have ever happen to me is to see sunshine, and to be with Cardinal when I do. Just then, he leans in to my face with his face, and he grew ever so close. I could feel his breath again, I closed my eyes, and our lips meet. It was the sweetest kiss ever. If sunshine were in human form, it would be Cardinal. He gently touches the back of my head with his hand, and I take my hand and place it on his shoulder. I can feel my whole body shiver, and I feel as if I never want this kiss to end. When our kiss ends, we hold each other for a long time without saying one word to one another. I finally tell him that it is getting late, and I have to go home. He decides to walk me halfway, and we push our slicker buttons and off we go. The rain is coming down hard, and the next thing I know, my slicker broke, and my hair is getting drenched. He quickly removes his backpack and throws it on me. His slicker smells like him, and I never want to give it back.

"Cardinal, you are getting soaked!" I scream. It is too late; he is wet from head to toe.

"It's okay, Bloom, when I get home, I'll sit in the drying room a little longer than usual." He explains.

CHAPTER SEVENTEEN

W HEN WE GET TO MY front door, we kiss quickly again, this time, it is not a long kiss, and he whispers in my ear, "I love you, Blooming Flower Rising."

I cannot believe this! "I love you too Cardinal Red Miller." I say while feeling so happy inside.

We both are grinning from ear to ear, and he turns to leave. "I'll see you tomorrow, Bloom!"

The next day at the Learning Center, everyone is excited. Today we are getting our seeds! Mr. Pelican, who is the senior Principal of the learning center, announces over the main G.C.I. the seeds are here, and each class will receive the seeds. Everyone will get a special pot, and the pots are small enough to carry in your backpacks, so you will need to carry them with you in case there is any sign of sunlight. If the sunlight appears while classes are in session, your instructors will lead you outside and you will stand in a row with each other, and place the pot in front of you. You are to place one to two seeds in the pot of soil, and push the seed down with your finger, and cover the hole up with the soil. The seeds will sprout within one hour to a full size flower, providing there is enough sunlight. As soon as the sun goes away, the flower will droop and disappear back into the soil, go dormant, and wait for the sun again". Everyone is busy talking, and getting excited. Everyone seems to be happy and smiling, and even Morning Glory looks my way at one point, and smiles at me. I think that this is a new beginning, this is going to bring all of us together, and we will all work toward making the Earth's future bright again. I picture Cardinal and me owning our own house together, and we have children running around the front yard. The sun is shining and we have a garden with flowers and vegetables.

My daydream is short lived because our instructor comes around, and everyone sits very still at his or her desks. He gets to me, and hands me a pot, a bag of special soil, and little black things. The label on the black things say "tulip".

Wow, I am going to grow a tulip! I cannot wait to see what kind of seeds Cardinal and Jaybird got! I cannot wait for the day to end.

The alarm goes off ending the learning center day, and I make my way through the crowd of students to first to find Jaybird, then hopefully Cardinal. Jaybird is waiting for me with a huge smile on his face.

"I got crocus seeds, Bloom!" He shouts, and lifts up his pot to my face as if there is something different to see from mine.

"That's great, Jaybird! Now let's find Cardinal, okay?" We head down the hall, and sift through the crowd. Everyone is meandering around showing off his or her seeds to one another. It makes it quite difficult to get through the crowd, and I keep looking back to make sure that I still have Jaybird following me. All the while, Jaybird is trying to talk to me as well.

"Bloom! I have to tell you something," he says as we maneuvered in and out of people.

"Not right now." I say, and I keep walking.

We finally get to Cardinal's class, and there he is standing there waiting for us. He has a big smile on his face too. "I got forsythia," He says. "I don't know what it is, but I bet it will be pretty, but not as pretty as you, Bloom." As he says it, he flashes me a big grin. I feel my face turn red. "Oh Cardinal, you are so sweet!" I gush. Jaybird is tugging on my sleeve, and still shouting that he has something to tell me.

"Okay Jaybird, let's go outside, and away from this crowd, and then you can tell me, Jaybird, okay?" All three of us make our way outside, and I finally feel like I can breathe again. "OK, Jaybird, what do you need to tell me?" I ask curiously.

"There is a new girl in my class, and she is very pretty, and her name is Snapdragon, and I like her, Blooming. I really like her. She is the prettiest girl in class, and she is very short, so the other kids in my class started making fun of her. There was an empty chair next to me, so she sat there. We talk all day, and one time, we almost got in trouble, but we did not. At lunch, I show her where we go to get our syringes administered, and she smiled at me a lot today! I cannot wait to see her tomorrow! I am going to ask her to stand next to me at the dance."

Jaybird's age group will have their own dance in another part of the learning center. It is a great opportunity for everyone to socialize and try to become friends and have a sense of community.

"I am very glad to hear that you have a new friend, Jaybird. I am also very proud of you for not making fun of Snapdragon. You know what that feels like, and it is not a good feeling, is it?"

"No, it isn't, and sometimes, I want to yell at the other kids when they start making fun of my scar on my head, but then I remember that Momma always says to turn the other cheek, and so I try to turn away and act like I don't hear them, but I do hear them. Bloom, do I look like a freak?"

"No Jaybird, and don't you ever say that about yourself again!" I say angrily. "You are alive to make a difference, and someday, God will reveal that purpose to you, you just got to have faith."

"Where is God?" He asks.

"He is everywhere, Jaybird." interrupts Cardinal. That makes me smile. I have never heard Cardinal speak of any kind of spirituality until now. In this moment, I know we are somehow going to be okay. We make it home, and Jaybird runs in to show Pappa his seeds. I kiss Cardinal goodbye on his cheek, and head inside myself.

CHAPTER EIGHTEEN

W HEN I ENTER THE HOUSE, everyone is in the common area, examining Jaybird's seeds. G- Paw and G-Maw are amazed that the seeds are so tiny.

"What kind did you get, Bloom?" asks G-Paw, and I pull out my seeds and hand him them to examine. "This is it, kids! This is the start of a completely new world! If we get some sunlight the weathermen predict, we can see flowers! Oh how great will that be!" shouts G-Paw. "I didn't think I would live long enough to see a flower again, but I just might!"

He throws his hands in the air, and even dances a bit around the couch. I have never seen him so happy before. G-Maw is sitting quietly in the corner chair, and G-Paw goes over by her and says, "If we get flowers, you are the first person to get a bouquet my love."

She looks at him with adornment, and then says, "You old crow! Now stop that." He pretends to tickle her, but she looks a little annoyed. I have never seen either one of them act this way. This is a change for everything and everyone. This is huge! I realize that our whole existence could change forever if sunlight returns. Someday I hope to have children, and I do not want them to know this way of life, or what it is like to receive all nutrition by syringes, instead of consuming food the way humans are suppose to. Maybe my children will have blonde hair. Maybe more people in the world will have blonde hair due to the sunlight, and I will not look so different. Maybe Doctors and scientists can finally find a cure for the terrible affects from sulfur, and no one will get sick anymore from it.

Just then, I realize that if the sun does come out, and there is no more sulfur, my Momma might lose her job if she can no longer sell gas masks. *Well that is way down in the future*, I think to myself, and then I decide to enjoy the moment.

That night, I dream that Cardinal and I are running in a field of multi-colored flowers. We come to a stop, fall to the ground, and the grass under us is as soft as carpet. We hold each other, and then in my dream, it starts to rain, thunder, and lightning. In the distant, I see a dark figure heading toward us. As the figure gets closer, I see that it is Morning Glory. She is running straight for me, with a large object in her hand as if she is going to swing it at me. As she starts to swing, Cardinal jumps in front of her, and she hits him instead by accident. He falls down to the hard ground, and blood is flowing from his head. I scream, and Morning Glory runs away into the dark lit field. Just then, the alarm system goes off telling me it is time to get ready for the learning center. I am shook up from my dream, but I am very thankful it is just a dream. As usual, I try to rush, throw on my uniform, and bolt downstairs to get the better syringe. When I arrived in the kitchen, Jaybird is not there. I administer my syringe to myself, and venture upstairs to find him.

He is in his sleeping quarters, talking to someone on his G.C.I... When I enter his room, I ask whom he is talking to, but he quickly shuts the G.C.I. off, and says, "Snapdragon, Bloom! Now if you don't mind, please get out!"

I laugh, and scurry out of his room. *My little brother has a crush on someone*, I think to myself. I shack my head and wait for him downstairs.

CHAPTER NINETEEN

WHEN WE ARRIVE AT THE learning center, Finch greets me at the door and says, "Hi, are you coming to help decorate again tonight, Blooming? We really need all the help we can get. The dance is just a little under a week away, and the decorations are not complete yet. If you do not want to paint, I understand. You can help build the centerpiece that is going up on the stage."

"I may be able to come and help, but I have to let my Pappa know so he can get my little brother," I say.

"Great! Thank you Blooming" He says, and walks away.

Cardinal approaches me, and says, "Are you going to stay after classes today and help decorate the dance hall? I thought I might if you do."

"Sure". I say. "I have to find my Pappa, and let him know my plans." I head off to find my Pappa and my Pappa is busy in one of the offices helping one of the learning instructors, and I proceed to tell him my after-learning center plans, and he says he will get Jaybird. After the learning center was over, I head to the dance hall and look for Cardinal.

"My goodness, "He is so handsome!" He makes my heart skip a beat when I see him. There is another girl talking to him. It is Narcissus, a petite pretty girl with long brown hair. Her hair has natural waves in it and as she speaks, her hair gently sways from side to side. She is smiling at him, and suddenly I feel jealous. I want to interrupt their conversation, but I know that would not be very polite. I have to get out of there for a moment and get some air, but Chrysanthemum, another girl in charge of decorations approaches me and says "Blooming if you are not doing anything, can you go to the west side of the building? There is a room down there called the developing room. That is where the photography classes go. The sensor lights will come on of course, but the room is still dark. There is some black linen down there tucked away in the corner of the room. We can really use to place on some of the tables up here. Please Bloom?"

I really want to get out of the hall, so I agree to walk down and retrieve the linen. I make my way to the west end of the building and realize that I have never been down in this area before. I find the room marked developing room. I open the door and the sensor lights do come on, but as Chrysanthemum pointed out, it is dark still. I fumble around to the back of the room, and as I feel around with my hands, I reach in a dark corner, and see the linens. I gather them up in my arms, and just then, the door slams shut. The room is now completely dark, and the sensors will not come back on, even though I am waving my arms furiously about. Still holding the linens, I feel my way to the door, and try to pull it open. As soon as I get the door to swing open, the sensor lights come back on.

You are a little late.

My arms are full as I make my way back to the dance hall. I run into the learning center custodian, Mr. Quail. He has been working there for as long as I can remember. He is a heavyset older man, and he has many wrinkles on his face, yet, he looks very kind. I remember he looked old to me even when I was a very young girl.

"Blooming, right?" he asked. "I recognize you because of your hair."

I stroke my hair with my hand, and try not to drop the linen with my other hand as he spoke, and say, "Yes sir".

"Where are you coming from with all those linens, and here, let me help you," he says, as he scoops up half the linens I had in my arms without waiting for me to answer his question.

"I got these from the developing room," I explain.

"Oh, that door didn't shut on you, did it?" He asks. "I've been meaning to fix that door. I know it closes by itself sometimes. One of these days, someone is going to be stuck in there, so try not to go into that room alone next time. The door shuts because the building has settled with all the rain after so many years and the building leans a little, just enough to make some doors on the west side of the building shut by themselves."

"Yes, the door closed and then the sensor lights would not come on." I say with a bit of a worried look.

He can tell I was a little aggravated, and maybe even a little scared. "Well, it's always good to go with someone in this building if you don't know where you are going. This is an old building, and things start to fall apart after time."

I guess I never thought about the Learning Center being an old building. I know my Momma and Pappa attended here when they were younger, so I guess it was an old building.

I make my way upstairs with Mr. Quail following close behind, and we enter the dance hall together. I find Chrysanthemum, and she orders me, and Mr. Quail to place the linens down on the table. Mr. Quail complies, tells me goodbye, and he leaves the hall. I look around for Cardinal, but I do not see him. I decide I have had enough fun for one day, and head home without finding him to tell him goodbye.

CHAPTER TWENTY

WHEN I GET HOME, AND head upstairs to my sleeping quarters, Cardinal is calling me on the G.C.I... I answer, "Hello? What do you need?"

He senses my aggravation, and says, "Why did you leave, Bloom? I looked everywhere for you. I was worried Bloom. I could not find you. The least you could have done was to tell me goodbye"

"I saw you talking to Narcissus, and then Chrysanthemum sent me on a wild goose chase on the west side of the building looking for something. When I got back to the dance hall, I did not see you so I decided to head home."

He can tell that I was angry, and a little jealous. "Blooming Flower! Are you jealous? She was asking my advice on something. She likes this boy named Hawk, and she wanted to know if I would talk to him for her. Bloom, you have no reason to be jealous of anyone. I love you and you only."

I feel so relieved and very silly that I have allowed myself to become jealous. I smile at him through the screen.

"I have something to tell you, Bloom. My Uncle Owl is moving us back to Ohio, but not until this August. I will be able to finish my learning center year here next year, then once I move, I plan on getting a job, and making enough money to move back here, Bloom. I can't live without you forever."

"What about attending a higher education center?" I ask. "You know that your Momma always wanted you to take business in a higher education center after graduating from senior learning center."

"I know," He says. "Things have changed now, but what hasn't changed is the way I feel about you, Bloom. You are my future now."

"Cardinal, I don't want to hold you back. If you don't go to higher education center, then you might regret it later in life, and I don't want you to resent me for that." I say.

"That has never been my dream, Bloom; that was my Mamma's dream. My dream is to be with you and live here in Hawaii. This is where the sun will shine first. This is where you are. This is where God will first kiss the Earth with His Mercy. This is where I belong. Until then, we are going to have a great time together, and I may have to be gone for about a year or so, but I promise that I will call you all the time on the G.C.I., and I will get a job, and I will move back. Then we will be together forever!"

I can tell that he really means it, and that makes me feel safe, and happy.

"I'm sure that my Momma just wants me to be happy, Bloom, and I know that she loves you too. She would have been elated that we would be together. We practically grew up together, so it was fate that we are together now." He says.

"People will make fun of you for having a girlfriend that has blonde hair. They will tease you the way they do me. I don't want that for you, Cardinal." I say.

"Do you really think I care what people say about me, Bloom? I could really care less. If someone does not want to be my friend because my girlfriend looks different, then that is their loss, and I am not going to waste any negative energy on them," He says sternly. "Now I have to go help my Uncle with my nieces, but I will see you tomorrow, okay?"

"Okay", I say, "goodnight", and we hang up.

CHAPTER TWENTY-ONE

THE NEXT DAY AS I approach my cube locker, Morning Glory steps in my way and blocks me from getting to my locker.

"Don't you have a cement block to climb under?" I ask sarcastically.

"I know you are not talking to me that way." She says as she shakes her finger closely to my face. I roll my eyes at her, and try to move around her. She holds up her arm to block my way, and stands in front of me, between my locker and me.

"Why do hate me so much?" I ask abruptly. "What have I ever done to you anyway?"

"I don't like your hair, and Cardinal shouldn't like you either. Cardinal is *my* boyfriend and he is going to be with me, not you! He deserves me, not a freak like you!"

"Are you listening to yourself, Morning Glory? That was years ago. He told me all about it. He does not like you, he never did. He likes me! So you need to get over it!" I get the nerve up to move around her, and as I do, she shoves me into the wall. I gain my balance, and I push her back. I push her so hard that she lands into the cube locker next to mine. She has this look on her face of amazement. I do too. I did not know I was this strong, but I am angry too.

She falls hard against the cube locker, onto her leg. She lets out a scream! "You broke my leg, you freak!" She struggles to stand, and tries to run toward the nearest first aid office, and I go to my next class quite pleased of myself for finally standing up to her, and thinking that she may finally leave me alone for the last time. I walk into class and start to take out my study G.C.I and Ms. Goldenrod comes over to me, and ask that I go down to the office. She received a call from the head principal to summon me down. I lower my head, gather up my things, and head slowly down to the office. Mr. Pelican greets me at the office door. Behind him is Morning Glory still holding her leg, and announces that she is in excruciating pain. The nurse from the first aid office is standing behind her.

Mr. Pelican says, "I understand there was an argument at your cube locker a few moments ago, Bloom. Is this correct?"

"No" I reply, "she would not let me get to my cube locker, sir."

"Did you shove her out of your way?" He asks.

"Yes sir." I feel no better than the bully telling on me does. I feel awful.

"Is this true, Morning Glory? Did you keep her from getting to her cube locker?"

"No, she is lying!" She shouts as she points to me. "She started this whole thing, and she should not be able to be here! She is weird, and nobody likes her. Her hair is different, and she needs to leave!" I suddenly feel very alone, and like an outcast, and a bully. I want to run out of his office, but I do not.

"Morning Glory", Mr. Pelican calmly says, as he addresses Morning Glory. "Your hair is curly, and not everyone's hair is curly, and that is what makes you special. Her hair is blonde, and that is what makes Blooming special." There are things about each and every one of us that make us different from one another, but we are all human, and that is what keeps us connected with one another. "Now I want you both to go back to class, but if there are any other incidents, then neither one of you will get to go to the dance, or possibly suspension from the learning center. I don't care whose fault it is, is this understood?" He motions the nurse to sit down, and file an incident report for our parents.

We both replied, "Yes, sir" and leave the office simultaneously. We do not look at one another, and I go down another hall purposely just to get away from her. I suddenly turn around just when she is about to turn and disappear around a corner, and I say sincerely, "Morning Glory, I'm sorry about your leg. She stops suddenly, turns and listens for a moment, then looks at me with a haunting stare, and says quietly" I will make you regret this day, Blooming, I promise you that!"

She quit holding her leg, and starts running toward me. I jump back to try to defend myself, but she stops approaching me suddenly because we both hear an instructor walking towards us. She stops, turns, runs down the hall, and disappears. I stand still, and make sure she is gone, and then I slowly and cautiously head to class. I pass a restroom, and I dart in quick. Tears flow heavy down my face, and I feel so scared, and so alone. How can anyone hate me this much? Why does she hate me! I splash water on my face, and I see my reflection from the mirror in front of me. I just want to fit in! Why can't I just fit in! I pound on the mirror, and I continue to cry. I am so scared of Morning Glory right now.

After the learning center alarm goes off announcing the end of the day, I go to retrieve Jaybird, to get us both home as quickly as possible. As I arrive at his class, he is standing there talking to a girl. *This must be Snapdragon.* She is a short girl, just like Jaybird described her, and she appeared to be of Asian descent. I cannot help but notice her beautiful hair, because it is streaming all the way down her back. She is smiling ear to ear as she talks to Jaybird, and he is smiling right back at her. They do not notice I am standing next to them for a moment.

I try to clear my throat loudly, and say "Time to go Jaybird."

He looks up and says, "This is Snapdragon, Bloom!"

Snapdragon looks up at me, and I look down to her. She says, "Nice to meet you, Jaybird's Seester."

I say, "You mean 'sister'."

"Yes" she says, and she repeats "Seester" again. We both smile. "I am happy to come and visit tonight at your resident." She says.

I look at Jaybird with a puzzled look. "I invited her over I think," he says sheepishly.

"Oh, okay." I say. "Well we need to be going. You know that if we are not home when Pappa gets home, he will worry. Bye Snapdragon, we will see you in a bit, and it is very nice meeting you." I grab Jaybird's hand, but he quickly jerks away.

"I don't need you to hold my hand, Bloom! I am older now!" I giggle to myself, and just keep walking.

The skies are more ominous than ever today. Oh, how I wish the sun would come out. I do not even know what I would do if it did.

CHAPTER TWENTY-TWO

THE RAIN GOT HEAVIER AS we walk.

"Jaybird, we will have to go into the drying room when we get home." The drying room is a heated room year round. There are extra clothing in there for the whole family, and there is warm air flowing. It feels good after being out in the rain so much. I like going in there sometimes and just think or daydreaming. When I go in there, I imagine that it is my personal rain forest, there are animals everywhere, and it is tropical. The history lessons explain how life used to be in Hawaii. Many years ago, it was sunny and tropical, and it was the number one spot in North America to vacation. Sometimes I sit in the drying room, I daydream of my family living here, I can picture the tropical forests filled with life, and animals, while the warm sunlight beams down onto the forest floor. I wish my Momma did not have to work all the time, and we could spend more time with her, but then I realize we might not have a house or syringes for nutrition. We have a nice house, and for that, I am grateful.

We walk into the house and Jaybird starts shouting, "I have a girlfriend! I have a girlfriend! And she is coming over tonight!"

Pappa comes in from the kitchen, and sees that we are soaked, and he sends us both to the drying room. We were soaked through and through, and it is a bit chilly. After we warm up and are nice and dry, Jaybird races out of the room to find Pappa and proceeds to tell Pappa about his new friend, Snapdragon.

"Can she come over tonight, Pappa? Please? I kind of already said she could," he says in his sweetest little voice.

"Only if she comes with one of her parents, Jaybird, because if you like her this much, we need to get to know her family, especially since they have not been in country for very long. I remember completing paperwork on Snapdragon. Now go call and inform her please, and then let me know what is going on. If I need to spruce up the place, I need a little bit of notice."

Jaybird runs to call Snapdragon on his G.C.I. I stay downstairs just to have a moment with Pappa. After about 15 minutes, Jaybird comes bouncing back into the kitchen, and explains that Snapdragon is bringing her Pappa. Her Momma is working, and will not be home until late. Pappa starts to prepare the house for company. I dive in too, gathering up anything that looks remotely like clutter. I then decide to head to my living quarters to daydream about Cardinal and me, which has quickly become my favorite daydream.

A short while later, I hear conversation coming from downstairs, so I run and grab my comb and guide it through my hair. Momma always says to comb my hair before I meet new people because most of the time it is a shock to people to see blonde hair, and at least if it is combed, there is not much anyone can say. I run my brush through, give one last glance in the mirror, and then head downstairs.

I can see that Jaybird and Snapdragon are out on the back patio playing with his fighter Jet of course, and Snapdragon's Pappa is standing, and talking to my Pappa. I approach them both.

"Toucan, this is my daughter, Blooming.," says Pappa."

"It is very nice to meet you, Hummingbird has told me a little about you," says Snapdragon's Pappa. It is sometimes strange to hear someone call my Pappa by his first name, Hummingbird. I only know him as Pappa. Snapdragon's Pappa is shorter than I am. I try not to stare down at him. He is very polite, and has a smile that reaches from one ear to another.

"I know what it is like to look different." He says. "In Asia, we are all the same height, but over here, we are very short, compared to everyone else, and people tend to stare at us. Over here, we sound different from everyone else as well, but in Asia, everyone talks the same. It is hard for me not to stare at everyone else, because, to me, everyone looks and sounds different than we do. It will be an adjustment for Snapdragon. I am so happy that Snapdragon is friends with Jaybird, he is very funny, and make her laugh. Her Momma, my wife, works for the Armies. She is a scientist, and is continually working to find a way to diminish the sulfur in the air. I do not know much about what caused Jaybird's scar on his head, but am I safe to presume it is cancer? Scientists, such as my wife, who work for the Armies are always inventing and testing different sprays that will remove the sulfur in the air. The different chemicals they invent for the Armies are all top secret, and my wife cannot tell me much. My, your hair is really blonde, just like Snapdragon described it"

I do think it is quite lovely on you, Blooming, and Snapdragon wants her hair color to be just like yours."

We all start laughing.

Jaybird and Snapdragon come inside and exclaim that they are hungry. Pappa goes and retrieves the dinner syringes. "Guests first, Pappa says as he passes the tray to Snapdragon's Pappa. Snapdragon's Pappa reaches for a syringe and proceeds to administer Snapdragon's syringe to her, and Pappa administers Jaybird's to him. Jaybird and Snapdragon gleefully hold still, and grins at one another.

I listen to Pappa and Toucan talk for hours, and finally, Toucan announces it is time for them to leave. We say our goodbyes to Snapdragon and her Pappa, and then it is time for all of us to head for bed.

CHAPTER TWENTY-THREE

ORNING COMES TOO SOON, AND I climb out of my bed and check the mirror. *Strange, all the science they have available, and they cannot find a cure for acne!* I take my fingers, and pick at my cheek a little, just enough to make it bright red, then head downstairs.

"Good morning!" greeted Pappa.

"What's so good about it?" I snap scornfully. Pappa takes one look at me, and then he sees it. He does not say anything, and I notice he is catching glimpses of me without being noticeable that he is trying not to stare. The pimple is too red to hide. *Today was going to be terrible,* and I head for the front door.

"Bloom, you get back here and wait for your brother please!" yelled Pappa. "You both come straight home after the learning center; Momma is going to call us via G.C.I. She has been assigned a new partner from her company, and Momma wants us to meet her tonight during the call."

As I walk outside, and wait for Jaybird, my backpack breaks as I push the slicker button, and of course, I get soaking wet. I go back into the house, and retrieve my reserve backpack from two learning center seasons ago, and, to me, it looks dorky. I get to the learning center, and there is a note on my cube locker via hologram. When I press play, it is of course Morning Glory, and the hologram only projects a picture for 30 seconds then it disappears. Morning Glory looks very mean, and vigorously shakes her fist at me in the image. This is the last thing I need today, and I immediately shut down the hologram, and head to class, feeling scared of Morning Glory, and self-conscious due to this big fat pimple on my cheek. I stay to myself for the remainder of the day, and when the end of day alarm blares, I cannot wait to get out of there, and head home to hide my hideously disfigured face from the now gigantic pimple on my face. I am sure it is not as bad as I think it is, but it just hurts, and feels huge to my finger when I touch it.

When we arrive home, I gather up some medicine for my face, and then wait for the family to come gather around the main G.C.I in the common area, and wait for Momma to call. When it finally rings, I feel excited to see Momma. It seems like forever since I have seen her. She appears on screen, and we all wave at her. She smiles and then introduces her new work partner, Aster Naumous. She is a stout woman, and she has a loud, fun laugh. It seems like anything anyone says, she laughs, almost uncontrollably. It comes across as a little annoying to me. My Momma looks good. She looks happy to see us, and to talk with all of us. She holds up the latest style gas mask with the newest bells and whistles it comes with. They all look the same to me. We all do our best to look interested in the conversation, and we always try to understand the details of the gas masks that Momma is telling us.

Pappa chimes in, "Rose, dear, will you be coming home this weekend for our anniversary? Did the company allow you time off?" He asks anxiously.

"Of course darling," She says. "I wouldn't miss our anniversary for anything, not even my work!" She exclaims.

My Pappa gazes at my Momma with love in his eye.

"How many years have you two been married?" I ask.

"Pappa and I have been married for what will be eighteen years, Bloom." says Momma.

Aster interrupts with a loud laugh. "That is a very long time!" She chuckles. I failed to see the humor in the conversation. I decide to wait to ask any more questions until my Momma comes home, and I can ask her and Pappa questions about their marriage face to face. We say our goodbyes, and as I turn to go upstairs, I notice Jaybird sniffling.

"What's wrong?" I ask.

"It will be days before we get to see Momma in real life!" Jaybird says.

"It will only be a couple of days, Jaybird, now let's get you upstairs and ready for bed."

He follows me slowly upstairs, and then he asks, "Do you think you and Cardinal will get married some day?" I stop mid step on the stairway, turn to Jaybird quickly, and say

"Why do you ask that, Jaybird?"

"Because I really like Cardinal, and I would like him to be my brother, since I don't have a brother, and I only have a goofy sister!" As he says this, he pushes on me jokingly.

"I don't know, Jaybird. Soon Cardinal will have to move to the province of Ohio, and we may not see him for a long time."

"I don't want him to move!" Jaybird shouts.

"I don't want him to move either, but he has to go with his Uncle Owl, and finish senior learning center next year. We can call him every day on the G.C.I. though, I promise. Now go to bed. Did you clean your mouth?"

Jaybird lowers his head, and says, "No, not yet." Ok, then, you head for the washroom.

The washroom is all push button. All you have to do is hold your mouth open, and with one button, the machine comes down and starts cleaning your mouth. You just need to hold still for a few minutes. I think the holding still part comes hard for Jaybird. After Jaybird finishes brushing his teeth, he says, "my mouth feels clean, Bloom. No dirt!" He opens his mouth to expose his teeth to me for reassurance. Pappa always tells Jaybird and me never go to bed with a dirty mouth. Dirt may just want to move in your mouth and stay. Jaybird says that he does not want any dirt to move into his mouth.

CHAPTER TWENTY-FOUR

THE DAY FINALLY ARRIVES. TODAY is the day that Momma is coming home to celebrate her and Pappa's anniversary. Pappa scurries about making sure everything is perfect. I was born in the year 2087, four years after. Pappa told me they had met in their last year of their senior learning center days. Pappa needed a tutor for language class, and Momma was a tutor. His parents acquired Momma to tutor him. Momma is a year older than Pappa. Momma has always been interested in science, and she always says she started selling gas masks to try to make Earth a better and safer place to raise her children. Back then, when my parents were younger, often times when it rained, there were terrible storms with an abundant amount of thunder and lightning. We do not see too much lightning any more, and we rarely hear thunder. I cannot imagine what a strong storm would look or feel like. I only know the constant sound of rain. In our syringes, there is a special kind of nutrition, to help us with sleepiness. The constant sound of rain will make you just want to sleep, but the nutrition in our syringes helps us keep our energy levels up throughout the day.

At least, it is warm outside. Some places of the Earth that used to be habitable, and saw climate changes such as seasons, is now uninhabitable and covered with snow, including all of North, and South Dakoda. Years ago, when the snow moved into that area, people had to migrate south, and leave their homes. Canada turned into a mountain range about eighty years ago due to earthquake activities. I have seen pictures of Canada; it was a fascinating place with one of the world's largest waterfalls called Niagara Falls. We studied it in learning center one year. The Elders say that once the fall froze, they knew it was the end for people to be able to live in Canada.

Momma calls and says that she is close to home, and only about half an hour away. We all hurry to clean ourselves up, and G-Maw, G-Paw,

Jaybird, and I are going to greet Momma for a few moments, then leave for the night to give Momma and Pappa an evening to their selves. We are all going to the air bowling facility across town. G-Maw and G-Paw are excited about going. They do not get out much anymore, especially with Jaybird and me.

Momma comes walking into the door, Jaybird jumped into her arms, and we all yell "Happy Anniversary!" simultaneously. Pappa gives Momma the biggest, longest hug ever, and then from behind his back, he pulls out the tiniest little beautifully wrapped box. Momma holds out her arms willingly, takes the box, and then gives Pappa a kiss on the cheek.

"Happy Anniversary, my darling." says Pappa. The way he looks at Momma is nothing short of admiration. By watching him, I can tell he loves her so very much and I can tell in every movement in his body, and tone in his voice. Momma looks at all of us and we are holding our breath, waiting impatiently for her to open that box!

"Aren't you guys all going somewhere?" she asks while she shoots G-Maw a stern look.

G-Maw looked at G-Paw, and says, "Come on, old man, time to go!"

G-Paw, Jaybird, and I all give out the heaviest sigh at the same time. "Aren't you going to open the box?" I ask.

"No, not right now, kids, now you all go off and have some fun!" says Momma.

We all head to the door, grab our backpacks, and head out into the rain. G-Paw and G-Maw are close behind Jaybird and me as we head toward the family vehicle. G-Paw programs in the bowling alley into the autopilot, and off we go.

CHAPTER TWENTY-FIVE

THE WHOLE NIGHT OUR G-PARENTS act like big kids themselves. They tease and taunt each other, trying to make the other one miss and mess up their bowling game. It is fun to watch them act like this. When we arrive back home several hours later, we all want to know what was in the box, but Momma and Pappa are in their sleeping quarters with the door shut tight. We did not even hear any noise come from the room, so we all go to bed as well.

The next morning, Momma and Pappa are dancing in the kitchen to some weird music via the kitchen speakers.

"What kind of music is this? I ask. "It sounds ancient!"

Jaybird comes running in the kitchen, and says, "I like this music!" and he gets in between Momma and Pappa and starts to dance too.

"Momma, what was in your gift box?" I ask. Momma motions us both to follow her to the living room, and she will show us. We sit around her, and she pulls out the box. She opens it, and it is something we have never seen before. Jaybird and I both say "Ohhhh!" at the same time. It is a rose petal, and it is a gorgeous color red. It is perfectly preserved in a glass encasement.

"Oh Pappa, wherever did you find this?" I say

"I sent away for it months ago, I had to pay it off before the company would send it to me. I really wasn't sure if I would get it in time, but thankfully, it was delivered two days ago"

"I don't want to know how much it cost, Hummingbird, just know that I love it, and I love you too" says Momma.

Pappa got a rose petal because Mamma's name is Rose. We have only seen pictures of a rose, but never anything as real as this petal.

"That is a beautiful rose!" Jaybird exclaims.

"It's not a Rose, dork," I shout", it's a petal, and a petal is just part of a rose!"

"Blooming Flower Rising!" Momma shouts, "You will apologize to your little brother right now, young lady! I do not want to hear you talk like that to him or anyone else"

I roll my eyes defiantly, and look at Jaybird. Where he is standing, Momma could not see his face, and he sticks his tongue out at me tauntingly. "I'm sorry…Jaybird." I hang my head, and start to tear up. I wipe my nose with my arm, and say, "Can I hold it, Momma, please?"

"Sure, but keep in mind to be very careful, and don't drop it" she says.

"No, please don't drop it, Bloom, I don't know how I would get another one!" says Pappa nervously.

I gently hold it and examine every inch of it. I can see veins in it, and I know that is how the water once flowed through the flower to help keep it alive. The petal is a brilliant color red, and there is just a little bit of black on the tip.

"Why is this black?" I ask as I point to the black tip.

"That is where it was starting to die before they could set it in glass to preserve the petal," says Pappa.

I close my eyes, and pretend that I am holding a real rose in my hand. The pedal looks as soft as silk. It looks so delicate.

"This is my favorite gift ever," says Momma. I am still holding it, and then, all of a sudden, Jaybird reaches up and tries to grab it out of my hand. I quickly jerk my arm away to keep it from him, and as I do so, the petal flies out of my hands, and luckily lands on a pillow on the couch. Pappa gently picks the rose pedal up, and as he does, he examines it for any damage, and then sternly points to the stairs, "Now both of you go upstairs to your sleeping quarters for a while".

Jaybird and I look at one another, and we feel ashamed, and head upstairs. As we walk slowly up the stairs, I look back and see that Pappa places the petal on the high shelve in the living area, and definitely out of our reach. I continue upstairs and decide to check my G.C.I. for any new massages. The upcoming dance at the learning center will be soon. There are not any messages, so I turn on a show, and watch it for a couple of hours, until time for bed.

CHAPTER TWENTY-SIX

T HE NEXT MORNING, JAYBIRD IS extra giddy walking to the learning center. He sings and skips most of the way there. As he skips, the water from puddles splash up on me.

"Stop splashing me, Jaybird! What is going on with you today?" I ask, while I shake off the rain.

"I get to see Snapdragon!" he yells as he jumps into a very large puddle, and it seems that the whole puddle aims right at me.

"That's great Jaybird, but please stays out of the puddles." I say. I feel exhausted already, and the day has not even begun.

We make it to the learning center, and I see Jaybird walk into class. I am in my history lesson in fourth period, and suddenly my instructor, Ms. Goldenrod comes over to me, and tells me that I need to go down to the office. *What now? I have stayed away from Morning Glory lately.*

I go down to the office, and there is Jaybird crying and rocking in a chair, and looking very scared. I quickly rush over to him, and say, "Who hurt you, Jaybird! Who is it? Tell me please!" As I speak, I stand him up, turn him from side to side, and examine his body for any injuries.

"I took it." He moans. "I took it and I broke it, Bloom! It's my fault, and now Mamma and Pappa will quit loving each other!" As he says this, he let out the most mournful cry ever.

I hold him in my arms, and say, "Broke what, Jaybird? What did you break? What are you talking about?" Just then, Pappa comes around the corner with Mr. Pelican. Pappa is holding the rose petal he had given to Momma for their anniversary, and it appears to be broken. The petal is dangling outside of its safely enclosed glass. Pappa has a very sad and disappointed look on his face. I stand up from leaning down and hugging Jaybird, and I reach out my hand out to touch the delicate pedal. It is so fragile. I gently touch it with one finger, and it feels like velvet. It is so soft! I never would have imagined a petal of a flower feeling so soft and yet so firm.

"How did you get this, Jaybird, and why would you bring it to the learning center?" Pappa says, as he cradles the petal in both of his hands.

Jaybird starts to speak, but it is hard to understand him. He is crying so hard that his words mumble together.

"Jaybird, calm down just a little bit so we can talk to you." I say as I touch his shoulder and try my best to console him.

"I wanted to show Snapdragon. I wanted to show her how beautiful it is, so I climbed on a chair, and reached up for the rose petal. I put it in my backpack, and I was just going to show it to Snapdragon, and then take it back home and put it back on the shelve. When Snapdragon saw it, she got so excited that she grabbed it, and it fell out of my hands, and went crashing to the ground…and….broke!" Then he buries his face in his hands, and starts moaning and crying again. I feel my eyes tear up as well, because I have never seen Jaybird this sad before.

"Pappa," Jaybird says", Are you going to quite loving Momma now?"

"Why would you ever say that Jaybird?" asks Pappa. "I will always love your Momma with or without this petal. She and you kids mean the world to me. This petal may be able to break, but I can always replace it. Momma, your sister, and you are irreplaceable. Jaybird, I understand that you wanted to show Snapdragon, and I know you are very fond of her, but you should not have gotten up on a chair, and brought the petal to school. I am sorry, son, but you will not be able to go to the learning center dance this year."

"No Pappa! Please!" Jaybird pleads.

"I'm sorry, Jaybird, you need to learn that it is not acceptable to take things that do not belong to you. Now, you and your sister gather your things up and head on home."

"Okay, Pappa." I say, but Jaybird hangs his head and silently follows me out. The walk home with Jaybird is a quiet one. I have never seen him this quiet before.

"Hey, Jaybird, there is a huge puddle! How about you go give it your best stomp?" I say, but he slowly passes the puddle by without saying a word. Now I know that he is very sad if he passes up a prime mud puddle.

Jaybird turns to me and says, "I just wanted to show Snapdragon, Bloom. I want her to like me, and I wanted to stand next to her, and ask her to be my girlfriend at the dance, but now I can't even go!" As he talks, he kicks through a large puddle, and the water goes flying through the air.

"It sounds like you really like this girl, don't you, Jaybird?" I say.

"I do, Bloom, but the other day, I was going to go up and talk with her, and as I got closer to her, she was talking to Duck, another boy in our class. Duck gave her a picture that he drew, and she loved it, and asked him to draw her another one. I thought if I showed her the petal that she might fall in love with me, and forget about Duck. Now she will never forgive me because she got in trouble, too. Her Pappa came and got her from the learning center before you got to the office. Now she will never like me, Bloom!" As he speaks, he looks at me with his big brown eyes, and I see the hurt he is feeling.

I scoop him up in my arms, look straight into his eyes, and say, "Now you listen here, Jaybird Soaring Rising, you are not a quitter, and you will talk to Snapdragon soon. She will like you no matter what. You are a very kind, and funny person. I have seen Snapdragon talk with you, and I see that she likes you very much. That ole Duck has nothing on you, little brother."

"Do you think Momma will be really mad at me, Bloom?" says Jaybird.

"I think she might be upset at first, but she will still love you, Jaybird." I say. That seems to ease his mind for a minute, and he does not pass up the next big puddle, and stomps in it with both feet. I know he will be okay.

We arrive at our house, and walk inside cautiously. G-Paw meets us at the door, and tells us that Momma had to leave and go back to work. She had left earlier in the day. She has not heard about the petal yet. At least, I hope she has not. Jaybird normally gets sad when Momma leaves for work, but right now, he seems a little relieved. I understand, and feel a little relieved for him as well. He did not have to face Mamma today. When Pappa finally arrives home, he is unusually quiet, and slips off to his sleeping quarters without saying too much to anyone. G-Paw administers the dinner syringes, and Jaybird is his quirky self again, as if nothing tragic has happened. I am glad to see him carefree and happy again.

CHAPTER TWENTY-SEVEN

WE CHATTED WITH G-PAW FOR a little while, and I decide to head upstairs to check on messages on my G.C.I. There is a message, and it is from Cardinal. He wants to know the colors I am wearing to the upcoming learning center dance so that he can coordinate his suit to match with me. I message him back and explain that I will be wearing sunshine yellow, so he can dress accordingly. Cardinal seems to be a little better since his Momma has passed away. He is a bit quieter when we are together, and I know that he is probably thinking about his Momma during those quiet times. I just like to be near him, and most of the time, we do not even have to talk to enjoy each other's company. His Uncle Owl is a nice enough man, but when I am around him, I catch him staring at my head. I know he is staring at my blonde hair. He told Cardinal that he has never seen blonde hair before, and he is Cardinal's Mamma's older brother, so he has been around longer, and still has never seen blonde hair. I never feel comfortable around people staring at me, and my hair. I always feel very comfortable around Cardinal, and he has never treated me any different from anyone else because of my hair color. He accepts me just the way I am. His ac is one of the things I love about Cardinal. He always seems to make me feel special, like I am the only girl around, even if we are in a crowded room full of people.

The next day, we both meet in the dance hall after classes. The dance is just days away and there are still so much to be done. There is more decorating and painting. There are streamers and pictures to hang on the walls and ceilings.

I run into Chrysanthemum as soon as we arrive, and she asks me to go down to the dark room again, to retrieve some old pictures that have been stored in there. Chrysanthemum explains that the pictures would go perfect with the theme in the dance hall. I agree to go get the pictures, but I do not want to go alone, so I stroll over to ask Cardinal to go with me. He agrees, and follows me down the stairs, and we head toward the west side of the building.

"I have never been over here, Blooming, how did you ever find this room?" He asks.

"Chrysanthemum told me how to get down here, but the door sticks sometimes, and there is not much sensor light in the room. The last time I came down here, I was stuck in the room, because the door would not open. I got a little scared, but luckily, I got myself out, and I ran into Mr. Quail, the custodian. Mr. Quail told me that the reason it is so dark in there is that a long time ago, the learning center used that room as a dark room to develop old film from videos they would keep in there. The room had to be very dark, and cool." He also said that the door tends to stick because the building is very old, and it has settled, making doors stick sometimes. He did tell me not to venture down here by myself again, so I'm glad you came with me, Cardinal.

"If it is cold in there, I'll keep you warm," says Cardinal, and he snuggles up to me and put his arm around me, as we get closer to the dark room.

"Now here is the door, Cardinal. I'll go in and look while you hold the door open to give me some light, okay?" I ask.

"Okay, but hurry up, this place gives me the creeps!" says Cardinal, as his body shudders. "I have goose bumps! Look, Bloom!" I see the little bumps on his arm, and I start to laugh.

I walk in the dimly lit room, and head straight back to the corner, where I was before, and there are the old pictures on the shelf where I thought they would be. There is a box of yellow streamers too, and I just know that the streamers would look great hanging from the ceiling of the dance hall. My arms are full, and I quickly forget to grab them. We head back to the dance hall, and Cardinal helps me carry our decorations.

There is music playing when we arrive in the dance hall, and it is looking very festive. Cardinal suddenly takes everything from my arms, places it on a nearby table, swings me around by my arm, and says, "Bloom, will you dance with me?"

I say "Sure", and he guides me to the floor. He twirls me around, and around. It feels like a magical moment, and when the music ends, I notice that everyone has stopped decorating, and has been watching us dance. Everyone claps his or her hands for our dance, and I feel like the luckiest girl in the world.

After the song, I thank Cardinal for the dance, excuse myself, and head to the washroom. I am in one of the stalls of the washroom, and feeling quite happy with my life, and suddenly the stall door forces open. It is Morning Glory! She swings her fist and tries to hit me in the face, and I dodge out of the way just in time. I stand up, and try to back away from her.

"I bet if you had a black eye, Cardinal might not think you are pretty anymore!" she says as she swings again.

I manage to duck out of the way again, and maneuver my way of the stall. I turn to face her as she is standing in the stall, and it looks like she is working up another swing. Just then, another girl named Zinnia walks in. Even though Morning Glory towers over her, she has a reputation of a girl that you do not mess with. My Pappa tells me that she has a reputation for getting in trouble for fighting other students in the learning center. She has lost both of her parents when she was a young girl, and has been shuffled around from family member to family member, until finally she wound up here with her aunt. I have seen her early in the mornings on the side of the learning center building smoking her Vapor, which is not permitted on the learning center property. Not many girls smoke Vapor. I always act as if I do not see her, and mind my own business.

Zinnia stands in between Morning Glory and me. "Get out of here while you can!" she shouts at me.

"Are you gonna stick up for this freak?" yells Morning Glory.

"She is not a freak, she just looks different, so what? Do you have a problem with people looking different? If you do, then you can pick on me, or try to anyway!" shouts Zinnia back at Morning Glory. Morning Glory backs down, and I quickly scurry for the door. I try not to act too shook up when I meet back up with Cardinal, and I quickly tell him I was not feeling well, and ask if he can walk me halfway home.

"Sure Blooming, I have to go home and study on my G.C.I. for a test tomorrow, anyway. As we walk home, I hold onto his hand tightly. Did you get your dress yet?" He asks. "Is it sunshine yellow like your hair?"

"Yes, it arrived this morning, my G-paw messaged me, and I can't wait to go home and try it on. Oh, Cardinal, we are going to have the best time at the dance. Did you happen to hear the weatherman this morning? They are predicting that the sun is supposed to shine for about an hour on the day of the dance! That would make the dance perfect! It would be wonderful to see and feel sunlight! The weatherman says that if it really happens and the sun does come out, it will be brief, and that the sun is not supposed to shine for another two or three years from now. If it does not come out the day after tomorrow, then we may have to wait for a couple of years, and you might not be here in Hawaii, and we will miss seeing sunlight together!" I say. Cardinal can pick up the fear in my voice.

"Don't worry, Bloom, we will see the sunlight together. It will happen this week I just know it. "He leans in toward me as he speaks, and all of my worries just melt away. Everything about him is so comforting to me. I imagine that seeing sunlight would give me that same feeling. I really do not know what sunlight is like, but I do know that the thought of sunlight makes me feel good, and so does being around Cardinal.

CHAPTER TWENTY-EIGHT

CARDINAL ENDS UP WALKING ME all the way home, and I get the nerve to ask him about how he feels about Morning Glory. "Bloom, she liked me when I was a little *boy!*" He almost sounds disappointed in me for even asking. I feel like a jealous fool. "I only have eyes for the prettiest blonde-haired girl in the learning center."

I wonder who that is for a brief moment, and then realize that I am the *only* girl that has blonde hair in the learning center. I realize he is talking about, and we both laugh. "I am really going to miss you when I move, Bloom, but I promise that I will contact you every day!" Cardinal says sincerely.

We both get quiet, and hold hands our hands tight together. He kisses me goodbye, and just as he is kissing me, it stops raining for a brief moment. We look up at the sky, and it really looks as if the clouds are parting.

"It is coming, Cardinal! The sun is coming!" I whip out my pot with my special seed in it and hold it up to the sky. Cardinal follows suit, and holds his pot up too. The clouds gather, and we both let out a heavy sigh.

"Goodnight Bloom, I'll see you tomorrow," says Cardinal, and off he walks as the rain starts up again.

I walk into my house slowly, and as I pass the G.C.I in the living area, the weathermen are talking about the prediction of the sun popping through the clouds the day after tomorrow. I squeal with excitement and rush upstairs to check my G.C.I. for any new messages. As I enter my room, I see my new sunshine yellow dance dress propped up on my chair. I quickly try it on. It fits like a glove, and I look at myself in the mirror. I am too busy admiring myself and I did not notice my Momma standing at my doorway.

"Momma!" I yell, and I fall into her arms.

"Don't mess up your pretty dress, and now stand back so I can take a look at you, Bloom." She says.

"What a beautiful young lady you are, my daughter! Do you feel pretty in this dress?" she asks.

"Oh yes, Momma, and I'm so happy to see you!" I grab her by her tiny waist and give her a big long hug. "You made it home in time for my dance!" I say excitedly.

"I told you I would not miss this for the world, and to be able to see you and Cardinal together one last time will be priceless." I know you will miss him terribly when he moves away.

"Oh, he is going to move back here in about a year, Momma. He told me so, and I'm going to be right here waiting for him!"

"Bloom?" Momma asks. "Does Cardinal talk about his Momma, because I miss her very much, and I'm sure he does too." I see her face getting flush as if she is going to cry. "I miss Larkspur, she was my best friend. Do not get me wrong, my new partner, Aster, is a hoot to work with, and she is very funny, and very smart, but I still miss my dear friend, and I see her in Cardinal whenever I look at him now. He has her big heart, and her eyes. I am very happy that you have feelings for him, Bloom."

"Momma, how do you know I have feelings for him? Did someone tell you something?" I say puzzled. I am wondering who is spying on me.

"I see the way you two look and talk with each other whenever he is around, and it is no secret, because that is the way you're Pappa and I used to talk with each other. Of course, I had to deal with a crazy girl that liked your Pappa at the time. Her name was Pansy Stewart. Boy, she was crazy about your Pappa, and would do stupid things to get his attention. One time, she jumped in front of a hover car, so your Pappa would have to save her. He did, and she swooned over him for months. One time she threatened me, because he liked me, and he did not like her."

I chimed in, "There is a girl named Morning Glory at the learning center that likes Cardinal, Momma, and she does stupid things to get his attention, too. Wow, maybe your friend Pansy and Morning Glory are somehow related!" My Momma bursts out giggling, she rolls around on my bed, and grabs me, and we wrestle and tease each other for a few minutes. "Now get your dress off, and hung up Bloom, and get yourself cleaned up."

"Momma, do you know what Jaybird did yesterday?" I am hesitant to bring it up, but I am so worried about Jaybird. I am worried about what Momma is going to say to him, so I feel like I have to ask.

"Yes, I know Bloom, and I know that he didn't mean to break my gift, but you do understand that there must be consequences to his actions. He took something that did not belong to him, and the results were not good. He will never learn if Pappa and I do not punish him."

"I know Momma" and I sigh heavily. "I just know that he really likes Snapdragon, and he wanted to stand next to her at his dance."

"There will be next year for your brother, but he cannot go this year." Momma says sternly. She stands up, blows me a kiss, and leaves my room. I blow her a kiss right back, and proceed to twirl my dress around one more time. I take it off, and gently put it away for the big day.

CHAPTER TWENTY-NINE

THE DAY OF THE DANCE is finally here, and I eagerly hop out of bed. I still have to go to learning center, but it is letting out early so all students can rush home, get ready, and return for the dance.

I throw on my learning center uniform, and rush downstairs to administer my morning syringe, and then rush back upstairs to get Jaybird up so we can get going. As I enter his room, his sensor light is on, but he burrows deep beneath his covers.

"Jaybird, get up! We have to get going!" I say as I jump on his bed and try to pull the covers back, but he holds onto them tight, and stays buried.

"I don't want to go!" He says. His words come out muffled, and it is hard to understand him, because his head remains under the blankets.

"Look Jaybird," I say, "I know this is hard for you, and I know that you wanted to go to the dance and stand next to Snapdragon, but you can't go this year. Snapdragon cannot go either, but Pappa says if you behave tonight that you can call her on your G.C.I. I think you should slip on your dance suit you were going to wear, and then call her. When she answers, tell her to put on her dress, and you both can pretend that you are both at the dance."

He poked his head out of his blankets ever so slowly. I think he liked that idea. "Okay, I'll get dressed." He says hesitantly.

"Okay," I say, "now hurry up, please!" I rush downstairs and stand by the front door anxiously waiting for Jaybird to come down, get his morning syringe administered to him, and grab his backpack, so we can start our walk to the learning center.

The clouds look weird as we take off walking. There is a strange feeling about this day. The sky does not look as dark as usual and the clouds are moving extremely fast across the sky.

"What's going on with the sky Bloom?" asks Jaybird as he walks and looks up.

"I'm not really sure, Jaybird, but let's hurry, the alarm is still going off, and if it stops, then we will be counted late for learning center. Anyone who is late today may get penalized and might not get to go to the dance tonight." I say, as I pick up my speed.

"Are you going to stand next to Cardinal?" He says as he struggles to keep up with me.

"Yes, I hope to." I say happily.

"If you two get married, and have a baby, what would you name it?" Jaybird says.

"I am not having any babies any time soon, Jaybird Soaring! I would have to have a really good job, and Cardinal better be prepared to take care of me and the baby while I work."

"What if Cardinal wants to work, and he wants you to stay home?" Jaybird asks.

"That is just unheard of Jaybird. You know that all Mommas go to work, and Pappas stay home." I say, correcting him.

We arrive at the learning center, and everyone seems excited. Students seem to be in a hurry to get to classes. Classes will also end at two- forty-five, instead of the usual time of three- forty-five. The dance will start at four thirty, due to the premonition of the sun coming out. The learning center thought it best if this momentous occasion does happen, their instructors can guide the students, and plant the seeds for the future, thus changing the world, as we know it. During the day, people are a bit antsy, and no one can sit still in their seats. Even instructors seem distracted.

During lunch break, I skip my syringe, thinking that I may look fat in my dress, and by the end of the day, my stomach is rumbling. I decided to administer my snack syringe I have stashed in my cube locker. As I approach my locker, Cardinal approaches me.

"Are you ready for tonight?" He asks as he touches my shoulder gently.

"Yes," I say with big grin on my face.

"Okay, then I will walk over to your house about three- forty five and we will walk back here together, and be here by four. The night skies arrive around six thirty, and hopefully we will get to see sunlight, and maybe even our first sunset together." He says.

I smile gleefully, close my cube locker, and wave goodbye to him, and I proceed to retrieve Jaybird from his class. As I get closer to his class, I see his classmates standing around him, and his so-called friend, Chickadee McGee, is taunting him again, and slapping his head, while he chants, "Mr. Sinkhole head!" Everyone is laughing and pointing at Jaybird, while they stand and watch.

I rush in between them both, and shout, "Chickadee McGee, someday, Jaybird's hair will grow, and cover his scar, and he will always be handsome, with or without hair, but you will always be ugly inside and out, you mean, big-nosed little boy!" Everyone stops laughing and starts to back away. "Get out of here, all of you! You all are nothing but a bunch of bullies, and you should all be ashamed of yourselves." "You there, Dusty Miller O'Bryan!" as I point to a tall, thin boy in the taunting crowd. "You are nothing but a spoiled little brat, who picks on your little sister, and makes her cry!" "And you there, Verbena Sans!" I point my finger straight at her face. "How dare you laugh at my little brother? My Momma gave you a free gas mask when you were sick last year!" Verbena quickly turns away, and walks down the hall, and away from the once taunting crowd. "You, Parrot Bradley, you talk too much in class, and I know that you are close to failing this year, so you need to concentrate on your lessons instead of wasting time laughing at my brother!" I say, as I point my finger at Parrot. He stops laughing, and looks at the other students standing around. As I point to each child, each child lowers its heads down in shame. "Let's go Jaybird; you don't need to hang out with a bunch of bullies such as these!" I say abruptly, and I grab Jaybirds hand in mine, and guide him away from the crowd.

"Thanks, Blooming. You are my hero. I do not think Chickadee was ever going to stop. I don't mind my scar and neither does Snapdragon, and to me, that is all that matters," says Jaybird, as he smiles at me.

"I am so proud of you too Jaybird. You are my hero, because you are so brave, and you survived your sickness, and you never gave up, and believed that you were going to beat your cancer and you are. You are well, and you are strong. I know that one day, Jaybird, you will do great things, and everyone you know now will look up to you." He appears to looks a bit calmer than before.

As we walk home, the clouds still look very weird, and as we walk in the house, G-Paw is very intrigued with the G.C.I. weathercast. He does not raise his head to look at us.

"It might happen this evening!" He shouts to us.

"The sun might come out! That is what they are predicting! I'm going to get my chair and sit outside in my chair, and wait!"

"No you are not!"

G-Maw shouts from across the room. G-Paw looks like a hurt little boy for a minute being caught doing something wrong.

"You are going to get *our* chairs, old man!" She flashes him a smile, and he jumps up and quickly goes to locate their chairs.

"What is going on?" asks Momma as she enters the room. "Has everyone gone mad around here? Come on Bloom, I will help you get ready for your dance, and then I will get the dinner syringes ready. Pappa is at the learning center, and will be chaperoning the dance tonight."

I feel a little hesitant and annoyed that my Pappa will be there, but I am used to him being around the learning center. I rush upstairs, taking two to three stairs at a time. Momma is coming up right behind me. I grab my dress, and start to get out of my learning center uniform.

"Bloom" says Momma" Let me fix your hair first, please. This is a very important night, and I want you to look perfect! I have always dreamed of helping you get ready for your first dance. Are you excited to be standing next to Cardinal?"

I reach for my hairbrush, and I hand it to her. I pull up a pillow to sit on the floor in front of her, and settle in so she can brush my hair. "I remember my Momma, your G-Maw brushing my hair." She says as she strokes the brush though my blonde haired locks. "G-Maw used to look a lot different than she does now. She was taller and strong. I used to think she was the strongest woman in the world. I still do. I am very happy that she and G-Paw live here with us. Family is everything, Bloom. Always remember this." She says. She continues and says, "I do not remember my Pappas parents. They both died a long time ago, when I was a baby. They must have been very nice, because when G-Maw talks about them, she always says good things about them.

"Now you mind your manners tonight, Bloom, and stand proudly next to Cardinal. Just remember, if you catch people staring at your hair, it is only because they might be jealous of you, and they do not know what it is like to have blonde hair. They might be curious and wonder what it might be like to have such unique looking hair. Be proud of what God has given you. He made us all special in his own way." I listen to every word my Momma says, and somehow, I feel that tonight will be very different from most nights.

CHAPTER THIRTY

I AM FINALLY READY FOR THE dance. Every hair is in place, and I feel so beautiful in my sunshine yellow dress. I eagerly wait for Cardinal to arrive, and Jaybird comes up and touches my sunshine yellow hem on my dress. It is very lacy. He then reaches up to touch my hair.

I jerk back and say, "No, Jaybird! You can't touch my hair, you might mess it up!" I try to say it in a nice enough way. I know he is feeling sad and I do not want to hurt his feelings any further.

He backs away, and says, "You look very pretty, Bloom!"

"Thanks, Jaybird." I say. I have never heard him say that to me.

Cardinal finally arrives and I start to slip on my backpack. My Momma stops me and says, "Here, I want you to wear your G-Maw's slicker tonight, Bloom. She wore it when she was a young woman about the age you are now, and she went to her first dance. It has a special pouch on it to hold your brush, and anything else you might want to take with you." I slip it onto my back, and I can smell my G-maw. It smells good. My G-Maw is a quiet woman, and does not ever say too much, but when she walks in the room and sees her slicker on me, she stands back, smiles, and tears well up in her eyes. "Blooming, my dear, you are stunning." G-Maw says.

"Blooming, you look beautiful," says Cardinal as he flashes me a smile as well. "I will have her home by ten tonight, Mrs. Rising."

"You make it nine-forty five, Mr. Miller." Momma says jokingly. Cardinal nods in agreement, and we head out the door.

CHAPTER THIRTY-ONE

CARDINAL AND I HOLD HANDS for most of the walk to the learning center, and I feel as if I am floating on air. Cardinal has a matching sunshine yellow suit on and he looks very dapper. "Cardinal", I say,

"I might have to fight off the other girls tonight because you look so good."

He grins at me and says, "I only have eyes for you, Bloom, you know that". I feel at ease, and give his hand an extra squeeze with mine.

We arrive at the learning center, and students are standing about everywhere. There is music coming from the inside where the dance hall is. There are flashing colored lights, and the whole room looks like a flower garden I have seen in old videos. It looks so magical. We walk in, and we pick out a nice spot to stand and talk. His friend, Cockatiel and my friend Daisy walk up to us. They, too, are holding hands.

"Great dance!" says Cockatiel, as he gazes and smiles at Daisy. Daisy has on a beautiful white and black dress, and her long brown hair is perfectly styled in a very cute up do.

Daisy glances at the dance floor, and tugs on Cockatiel's arm. "Let's dance!" she says, and she drags him into the dancing crowd, before he gets a chance to respond.

"Do you want to dance, Bloom?" asks Cardinal.

There is a slow song playing, and I say, "Sure". He swirls me out to the floor, and scoops me up in his arms. We sway slowly to the music and we stare lovingly into each other's eyes.

Pappa comes up behind us, and says, "You both need to move just a little apart from each other." He pushes us gently away from each other with his hands. "By the way, Blooming, you look breath taking, and I love you very much," says Pappa.

I feel my face getting red with embarrassment, and say, "Thank you Pappa, we are just dancing, don't you have someone else to watch? Look Pappa, how about that couple over there?" and I point across the room.

Pappa sees another couple dancing too close according to his standards, and starts to head that way. He suddenly stops, and brings me close to him, and whispers in my ear "You are as beautiful as your Mamma, and I am so proud of you Blooming Flower." Then he leans in and says something to Cardinal, and they both share a smile and he walks away.

"What did he say, Cardinal?" I ask.

"He asked me to take care of you tonight, and to accompany you home safely." Cardinal says, sounding very proper as he speaks. "And tell me, kind sir, how did you respond to my Pappa?" I ask in my most proper voice I could summon inquisitively. We continue to dance until the music ends. The music stops playing, and without either one of us noticing, the two of us continue holding each other while swaying back and forth and staring into each other's eyes.

"The music stopped!" shouts Cockatiel from cross the room, and we both look at each other, look around the room, and notice everyone is staring at us. We chuckle at each other, and start to walk back over to our spot we were standing at before. We are in conversation with a small group of friends also standing near us when Daisy walks over to us, and Chrysanthemum is walking close behind her. "Blooming, can you come over here with us for a second, please?" Daisy asks while she motions with her hand for me to follow. They guide me away from Cardinal. He is engaged in conversation with another one of his friends, anyway. I follow the girls over to the other side of the dance hall, and they show me a strand of broken streamer. "Can you go down to the dark room, and see if you can find any more streamers that we can hang? We want the hall to look nice throughout the evening." Daisy asks.

"I remember seeing some yellow streamers down there!" I say excitedly. "I don't want to go by myself though, it is dark, and the door tends to stick."

Just then, Morning Glory, who was standing rather close to us, overheard our conversation and interrupts, "I can go with you, Blooming.

I will hold the door open for you; I know it sticks. I know the room you guys are talking about."

I give her a puzzled look.

"I'm sorry for everything that has happened between us, and I am so ashamed of how I have acted lately," she says. I look at her with amazement. My mouth is hanging open so wide that a small plane could land in it. "I have seen the streamers, and if you want, I'll get the streamers and you hold the door, okay?" She says.

I look around and see that Chrysanthemum and Daisy are eagerly awaiting my answer. "Please, Blooming!" asks Daisy. "This is a special night for all of us; it can't look special with tattered streamers. Besides, we have all heard that the sun might come out today, and that time is getting close. If it happens, then there will be nothing better to set that off than a yellow streamer that is not tattered!"

"Okay, okay!" I say, giving in to their demands. "Morning Glory, if you go with me, then we can get this done quickly, so let's go." Daisy and Chrysanthemum jump up and down, give me a quick hug, and then skip away to investigate the other parts of the dance hall to make sure perfection is present. I look at Morning Glory, and motion her to follow me.

As we walk, we are both quiet at first. We hit the long stairway leading down to the dark room, and she says "I'm over Cardinal; I just want you to know. I like another boy now. His name is Finch."

"I know him, Morning Glory; he is a very nice guy! I'm very happy for you, and I just want us to be friends." I exclaim happily.

"Can I touch your hair, Blooming?" She asks as her hand got ever so close to my head.

"I guess so, it feels like everyone else's hair, I think." I say. I do not go around asking people if I can touch their hair all the time. As she leaned in, I think she was also trying to smell my hair. I can hear her sniffing heavily. I get a weird vibe, and I slowly back away.

"It feels soft, just like I imagined it would." She says.

CHAPTER THIRTY-TWO

W E FINALLY ARRIVE AT THE door of the dark room, and I just want to get the streamers and head back up to the dance as quickly as possible. I am not even sure if I had told Cardinal where I was going, and I am feeling anxious anticipating to dance with him again. I know he would be moving soon, and I want to spend as much time with him as possible.

"I'll go in and you hold the door, Blooming." Morning Glory says. She starts to walk in the dark room, but hits her head on the ceiling because she is so tall.

"Ouch!" she yells as she holds her head and checks for any bleeding.

"Stay here and hold the door, okay, Morning Glory? I know exactly where it is, and I am shorter than you are. I don't want you to hurt yourself anymore." I explain.

"Okay", she says, she props open the door, and I slowly enter the dark room. It takes a minute for my eyes to adjust to the darkness, and I looked back to make sure I could see the door still being held open by Morning Glory. I confirm the open door, and I venture further to the back corner where the streamers are. I get to the streamers, scoop them up, and turn to head back toward the door.

As I approach the door, Morning Glory lets out a terrifying cold laugh, and screeches, "Now I will have Cardinal all to myself, you freak! You can stay down here and rot for all I care!" She swings and hits my head with something, and I fall to the ground. My legs have given out from underneath me, and I am dazed. The door shuts as I try to stop her and the door, but my head is hurting, and I can feel the warm blood streaming from my head wound. I lay back down in the darkness of the room.

I pound on the door, and scream, "Let me out Morning Glory! You get back here, and let me out!"

SLAM…SLAM…SLAM….

My hands are getting sore, and I feel around on my head, and discover a very large bump rising on my head. I try to stand, but I feel dizzy. I slide down the wall of the door into a heap on the floor, and start to cry. My eyes adjust a bit from the darkness, and I start to look around. I scan the room for anything I can possibly use to try to free myself from the room. I listen very carefully with my ear pressed up against the door to see if I can hear anything. I listen for a possible footstep. Maybe Mr. Quail will come down this way again. My mind goes to Cardinal. Oh, how I wish I could let him know I am down here. He will come and rescue me.

When my Pappa finds out what Morning Glory did, she will be in so much trouble. Then I realized these thoughts were probably not helping me in my current situation.

CHAPTER THIRTY-THREE

I DO NOT KNOW HOW LONG I have been in this room, but it feels like at least an hour. My guess would be the time is around five thirty or so. My head is pounding, but it feels like my head has stopped bleeding. The lump on my head is still quite prominent and starts to worry me. I try to touch it gently with my finger, but I have to pull away. It just hurts too badly. The dark room is still, yet my imagination gets the best of me, and it appears there are things moving in the darkness. "It is not real!" I yell aloud. "Get a grip!" I struggle to squint into the room, trying to spot anything that might be of use for me to escape this room, and go seek help for myself. I try to look for something I could wedge open the door with to try to open it. Somehow, I have to find a way out of the cold, dark room. If my calculations are right on what time it is, and the sun does appear, I cannot miss it. I have waited so long to see and feel sunlight.

In the meantime, Cardinal is realizing he has been talking with his friends for a while, and he decides to look for Blooming. By now, he is frantic, because it seems that he has looked everywhere, but cannot find Blooming. It has been more than an hour since he has seen Blooming. Cardinal asks every girl he comes in contact of to ask if anyone has seen Blooming, but everyone he asks answers "no". He starts to look for Mr. Rising, and as he turns a corner heading back towards the dance hall, everyone starts to head outside. Cardinal follows everyone in hopes to run into Mr. Rising. Cardinal glances back through the dance hall, which is now empty, one last time for Blooming.

I'll go see what is going on, I hope there is nothing wrong with Bloom. With that thought, he runs quickly outside to find Mr. Rising. When he hit the outside doors, to his amazement, it is not raining; in fact, the air is thick and warm. He looks up at the sky, and so is everyone else. Then it happens! The clouds turn almost white, unlike the usual dull grey color they constantly are. A brightness begins to occur in the sky, and all around. For a brief moment, Cardinal thinks this is the end of the world. Some students and instructors start to cry, and drop to their knees. They bury their heads in their hands. Cardinal keeps looking up and slowly but surely, he feels the sunlight on his face for the first time. It is so warm, and inviting. There is no more rain, and the warmth of the sun feels like his favorite blanket that his Momma wrapped around him when he was cold and a young boy. All the students realized what is happening, and one by one, starts to pull out their special pot and seeds from within their backpacks. They place them one by one on the ground, secure their seeds safely in the soil, and stare at their pots. Cardinal cannot believe his eyes. He looks around, and no one is saying a word. The crowd of students and instructors were silently watching the pots of seeds. The sky is blue, a brilliant blue. The clouds look like soft cotton balls that can be touched with an out stretched arm... The sun is a glowing orange yellow ball high in the sky. Cardinal starts sweating in his suit, but stays focused on the crowd for any sign of Blooming. Several minutes pass, and the crowd starts to cheer. Their seeds are blooming into flowers. There are so many different kinds. The flowers emerge out of the soil like little soldiers. The fragrance of the sweet-smelling flowers fills the air, and the sulfur smell is gone. Small delicate purple flowers come sprouting out of the pot belonging to the girl standing next to Cardinal, and the flower stem soars high toward the Sun. The stem has brilliant green leaves. Cardinal watched the pot, and now he is even more frantic to find Blooming, because she might be missing all of this, or in trouble and needs his help.

"Blooming! Where are you? He shouts into the silent crowd. "She is missing this! I have to find her! Has anyone seen Blooming Rising? " He starts to head through the crowd, and approaches Mr. Crow, the principal of the learning center.

"Mr. Crow! I can't find Blooming Rising!" He shouts to Mr. Crow.

Mr. Crow is too busy watching his own pot and flower, and without looking up, he says calmly, "I'm sure she is here somewhere, Cardinal. Now go back to tend to your flower; the weathermen did not know how long this event would last, and I do not want to miss a minute! My great

G-parents were the last in my family to see sunlight, and flowers, and now I get to experience this in my lifetime. I have waited for many years to see this happen, so I am not missing this, Cardinal. This is history in the making!"

Cardinal starts getting frantic and grabbing people, and shouts at them, "Have you seen Bloom? You know, the girl with the blonde hair!"

He finally makes his way over in the west corner of the building, and sees Mr. Rising, who is frantically looking for Blooming too. "Have you seen Bloom, Cardinal? I need to find her to experience this with her. Where is she standing with her pot?"

Cardinal gives him a very worried look and say, "I can't find her, Mr. Rising! I have looked everywhere."

Together, Cardinal and Mr. Rising head over to the women's room, and the empty dance hall. Mr. Rising proceeds to go into the woman's room, to check for Blooming, and Cardinal stands guard blocking any girls who try to enter while Mr. Rising is in there. Seconds later, Mr. Rising emerges quickly, and Cardinal can tell on his face that Blooming is not in there. The pair starts to run across the dance floor hall, and the music is still playing, and the lights are busily flashing for an empty room.

Morning Glory suddenly appears in Cardinal's path, and demands, "Would you like to dance with me Cardinal? We have the whole dance floor to ourselves." She points to the empty dance floor. She leans towards Cardinal and immediate takes her hands and grabs his hands and tries to lead him out to the floor. Cardinal suddenly realizes that Blooming and Morning Glory had gone down to the dark room earlier for streamers.

"It was *you*! Where is she? Where is Bloom, Morning Glory! What have you done with her?" Cardinal shouts. He jerks his hand away from hers and becomes very angry. Every vein in his face is popping out with frustration, and Morning Glory stands in front of him, and smiles.

She reaches behind her back, and calmly says, "She is gone, she left, and she went home. She told me to tell you she is not feeling well. At least that is where she said she was going. I told her that you and I were going to be together from now on, and she understands Cardinal"

"I don't believe you! Bloom would never leave this dance! She would never leave me without telling me goodbye! Where is she?" He shouts as he neared her face and from behind her, she pulls out a laser gun and holds it up to Cardinal's face. Mr. Rising dives into Morning Glory, and grabs the laser gun quickly out of her hands. He and Cardinal quickly subdue her on the ground.

"Come see the sunlight with me, Cardinal!" Morning Glory pleas as she tries to struggle free, but Cardinal and Mr. Rising hold her down tightly.

Mr. Rising pulls out his portable G.C.I. and calls for the authorities to come for Morning Glory. Cardinal remembers Daisy and Chrysanthemum talking to Blooming earlier, and he remembers the request they made to her about retrieving new streamers to replace the torn ones hanging loosely on the ceiling "That's it!" he shouts aloud. "I know where she is, Mr. Rising! I have to go to her!" Cardinal takes off running down the stairs towards the dark room, while Mr. Rising held onto Morning Glory until the authorities arrive.

Cardinal runs through the empty halls of the learning center, down flights of stairs that seem to go down forever into the west side of the building.

Meanwhile, I am still frantically looking for a tool to get myself out of this dark, cramped, musty-smelling room. My dress feels soiled, and tattered. I reach out into the dark with my hands to try to retrieve a potential tool I can use to escape the room. I find a long wooden plank on the floor, and lift it up with both hands. I try to wedge it between the door and the wall, but it snaps, and I go crashing to the ground.

"Ouch!" I yell, and I slowly stand back up.

I remember what my Momma has taught me years ago when I was trying to learn how to ride a hover board by myself. The board was quite difficult to maneuver, and it took a lot of practice to be able to stand on it while in flight. It took coordination, and determination. One time, I fell off the board hard. I stood up after falling off that board, and said, "I give up! I'll never learn how to ride this thing!"

"You do not ever give up on anything, Blooming Flower Rising! Once you give up, that is it! Game over! You are not a quitter, you will learn to adapt to this board, and if you teach yourself to ride this board, then you can teach yourself anything! Now come over here and get right back on it!" Momma shouted.

I want to give up, and lay in the dark, on the floor for a moment, but I remember my Mamma's words piercing my head. I slowly stand up, look around, and see what appears to be a piece of old metal rod. The rod is heavy, and pointed on one end. I brace myself and wedge the pointed end of the metal rod in the door, and the other end of the rod; I position it against the adjoining wall. I pull on the flat end of the heavy rod, and push on it with my weight, and, with a loud crack, it opens door enough for me to climb out! The light from the hallway hurt my eyes, and it takes a few moments for my eyes to adjust. I have been in the dark room for a long time. I shield my eyes with my hands as they adjust. I see a figure running towards me. It is Cardinal, and he yells my name, and comes running to me, scoops me up in his arms, and holds me tight for a moment. Then he pulls me away to examine me, and says, ""Bloom, I was so scared I wouldn't see you anymore! I thought Morning Glory hurt you! What happened to your head? You are bleeding! Did Morning Glory do this to you? I shake my head "yes" and I hold him close to me. "It's Okay now, Blooming. She cannot hurt you anymore. The authorities have her in custody as we speak. He looks at me, brushes my hair out from my eyes, and kisses me on the lips. My whole body tingles down to my feet, and my head temporarily stops hurting. Pappa suddenly appears around the corner. He is breathing quite heavily from running down the halls looking for me.

He reaches me, and cries, "Are you okay?" He sees my head and holds me away from him. Pappa proceeds to examine my body, turning me slowly, to make sure that there were no more cuts, bruises, or blood.

"I'm okay, Pappa. Morning Glory did this. I thought she changed, and she had decided to be my friend, but she lied to me, hit me on the head, and locked me in this room. Is the dance still going on?" I ask, as I look at both of them, and still feeling a bit dazed.

"Oh my gosh, Bloom!" yells Cardinal. "We have to go! The sun is out!"

"What!" I scream. "What do you mean, the sun is out? What's going on?" I reply.

Cardinal does not explain, lifts me in his arms, and starts running back upstairs. The hallway seems so long, and I cannot believe this is happening. I am so excited to see sunlight! *This is it! This is really happening!* It seems to takes about ten minutes to get back to the dance hall, and as Cardinal reaches the top of the stairs, the hall is still dark and eerie and the music is still playing to an empty room. He dashes across the floor, with me still in his arms, and pushes his way through the crowd standing outside. We reach the outside, and I notice everyone is starring down toward the ground, and in front of every student, and instructor, there are his or her pots. Cardinal gently puts me down on the ground, and I look up at the sky. I feel the sprinkling of rain, and the skies are quickly turning from a blue hue to a grey color. The air is lighter than usual, and the smell of sulfur is faint.

CHAPTER THIRTY-FOUR

THE RAIN IS FALLING FASTER, and everyone starts to pick up his or her individual pots, and marvel at the flowers that have grown before their very eyes. I turn to look at Cardinal, and he is weeping with his hands buried in his face. There is no trace of sunlight, and the sun is no longer visible.

I start to shake my head from side to side, and cry, "It's gone, isn't it?" I look at Pappa to comfort me somehow. "Did I miss the Sun? Pappa, will it come back?" I plead with him, while he holds me, and tries his best to console me. I grow silent. I look around at the flowers, and as I look, Cardinal approaches me with a brilliant yellow flower. "This is called a sunflower, Bloom."

I look at it through my tears, and reach for the pot, staring at this amazing living thing in front of me. I reach out and gently touch the petals. How soft they feel on my skin. I look at Pappa, and he is weeping uncontrollably. I glance at him, and try to give him a comforting look. Then Zinnia comes over towards me holding her pot with her multi colored flower in it. She gently takes the pot, lays it at my feet, turns quietly away without saying a word, and walks slowly back toward the building. All of the students are still standing in the rain, and is now staring at me. They are looking at my torn, dirty dress, and at my hair covered in dirt and grime from the floor of the dark room. They see my injured head, and the dried blood that has ran down the side of my face. I try to smile at Zinnia, but I too, do not say a word. There are no words to say. I have missed the sun; the one thing in my life that will change my life is gone. The one thing I have waited to see all of my life can only live within my imagination once again. Daisy slowly approaches me, and lays her flowerpot at my feet. She does not utter a word, turns, and slowly walks into the building, and out of the rain. One by one, all the other students, and adults bring me their flowerpots. Everyone moves silently, while all of these magnificent flowers are surrounding me. I look over towards the entrance of the learning center. I see Morning Glory surrounded by the authorities with her head down, and her hands handcuffed behind her. Everyone is silent as they stood in line to approach me, and one by one, they lay their flowerpots down before me. The fragrance from the flowers engulfs my senses. I envision myself in the sunlight that has disappeared, and the all too familiar black clouds emerge again, making the Earth dark once more. The flowers are starting to wilt back from the heavy rain beating down upon them, but their blooms fight for another minute of life above the soft dirt, before they retrieve back into the ground indefinitely.. I finally have my flower garden at my feet.

The End

Edwards Brothers Malloy
Thorofare, NJ USA
November 10, 2016